# BEYOND
### *the*
# FROZEN
# HORIZON

*Nicola Penfold*

STRIPES PUBLISHING LIMITED
An imprint of the Little Tiger Group
1 Coda Studios, 189 Munster Road,
London SW6 6AW

Imported into the EEA by Penguin Random House Ireland, Morrison Chambers,
32 Nassau Street, Dublin D02 YH68

www.littletiger.co.uk

First published in Great Britain by Stripes Publishing Limited in 2022
Text copyright © Nicola Penfold, 2022
Cover image © Kate Forrester, 2022

ISBN: 978-1-78895-447-1

Printed and bound in the UK.

The Forest Stewardship Council® (FSC®) is a global, not-for-profit organization dedicated to
the promotion of responsible forest management worldwide. FSC defines standards based on
agreed principles for responsible forest stewardship that are supported by environmental, social,
and economic stakeholders. To learn more, visit www.fsc.org

10 9 8 7 6 5 4 3 2 1

# BEYOND the FROZEN HORIZON

## Nicola Penfold

**LiTTLE TiGER**

LONDON

*For the eco-activists*
*and the wonder seekers*

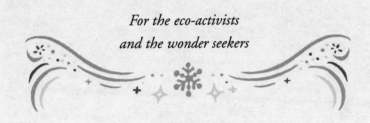

# Background

In 2030, world leaders pledged a coordinated and unprecedented response to the Climate Crisis. Global Climate Laws were brought in, including a ban on the extraction and burning of fossil fuels, stringent targets to reduce the consumption of meat and dairy products and a ban on single-use plastic. World Wilderness Zones were also established, setting aside vast areas to absorb carbon and act as vital wildlife refuges. For the first time in history, wildlife was prioritized over humans and people were moved out of the Wilderness Zones. The High Arctic was one of these designated zones and included the archipelago of Svalbard.

Temperatures have continued to rise, but there is hope that the rate of warming has slowed.

# Flight

I'd never been in the sky before.

It feels unnatural. A subversion of all the laws of physics, and all the Climate Laws too. Humans don't belong in the air.

But I hadn't reckoned on the excited twitch of my brain as the metal cylinder hurtled into the sky. Above the clouds, looking down on England as we left it behind for six whole weeks.

The box-like shapes of Mum's and my estate, with its new build apartments and neat green spaces, and my sprawling academy school, glowing in the early morning light. Then more town buildings – the leisure centre, supermarket, hospital, sports stadium – and roads whirring with electric cars, until a swathe of green, like someone got a paint pot and threw it over the earth's surface. One of the new forests, to suck up carbon and give wildlife a fighting chance to recover. The trees are a collage of shades and textures, in different brushstrokes – alder, cherry, maple, birch, willow, hawthorn. Somewhere in the tangle of trees is Dad's wooden hut with a solar-panelled roof and a tiny annex that's mine every second weekend.

I pull myself away from the window. A book's open on the table in front of me. *Creatures of the Far North*. It was Dad's gift to me for the trip, alongside a Polaroid camera that's sunshine yellow and little boxes of film. "To capture your adventures," Dad had said. He doesn't trust phone cameras.

"How are you feeling, Rory?" Mum asks beside me. "Six weeks in the Arctic! It's quite something, isn't it? I hope we're doing the right thing taking you out of school like this."

I let the words drift over me. "It's only Year Eight, Mum. It's not like I have exams or anything."

"You must still do the work you were set. I promised Ms Ali…"

Typical of Mum, to start up about school when I'm strapped in and there's nowhere to run to. Does she expect me to have a textbook out instead? It's not like I'm behind. It's not the work that's a problem for me at school.

I close my eyes deliberately.

Mum squeezes my hand. She whispers, "I'm sorry.

We can sort it out later. Maybe you need a break first, time to reset your brain, switch off from all that."

Neither of us wants to acknowledge what "that" is, but behind my eyes there's a crowd of faces and taunts. That I'm strange and quiet. That I don't belong. That I should run away with my dad to the woods. Mum swears I could fit in at school if I try, but I don't seem to know how. It was different when I was younger and we lived in a line of terraced houses with parallel back gardens and my best friend in the whole world next door. Betty. Every morning we walked to school together, Dad waving us off with a smile.

Those houses are gone now. Our primary school as well. They were too old and draughty to bring up to new energy efficiency standards. Or, if you believe my dad, developers moved in waving green home grants and thick wads of cash. Either way, the wrecking ball came and the rubble was repurposed into apartment blocks.

Betty's parents got jobs at one of the nuclear plants and moved out to the coast. We moved to one of the new estates. A two-bedroom cube of convenience on the tenth floor, with a tiny balcony and a couple of planters as outside space. Dad said it was bad for his soul, growing herbs in the sky, hearing neighbours through the walls. He said there wasn't enough oxygen. He and Mum became angrier and angrier with each other until neither of them could stand it. Dad found a job as a ranger in one of the new forests that came with its own place to live.

Sometimes I take a bus back to where our old street was. It's nice enough – there are reed banks and wildflower beds, bird feeders and children's playgrounds. But I'll never stop feeling sad about our old house. The back garden had a tangle of shrubs with a hidden space inside. Betty and I would lie there for hours listening to birdsong and the hum of the bees, being visited by neighbourhood cats.

"What are you thinking about?" Mum asks now, scrutinizing my face.

"Just school, I guess," I say.

She squeezes my hand and stretches her legs out under the seat in front. Her face breaks into a sudden grin. "I can't believe we're doing this. You and me, girls together. We're going to the far north, Rory. To the land of bears and ice and lights!"

"I thought you said it was going to be twenty-four-hour darkness!" I can't resist saying. We'll be arriving in the countdown to the polar night. Every day shorter than the last until the sun won't rise at all till spring.

Mum laughs. "We have a few weeks of light first. Plus we'll have the northern lights. The *aurora borealis*! We're sure to see them, spending all that time on Svalbard."

"*Aurora borealis*," I repeat, enjoying the way the vowels feel in my mouth. Then "Spitsbergen," I say, emphasizing the consonants in the name of the largest island in the Svalbard archipelago. It's going to be our home for the next few weeks, in an old coal mining town that Mum's new company, Greenlight, is reopening to extract rare earth metals. Silvery grey elements, magnetic and electrical, that make things faster, stronger, lighter, smaller. Batteries, wind turbines, electric cars, smart phones, cancer drugs – there's a rare earth metal in all of them.

"Spitsbergen," Mum says. "Hard to say without spitting!"

I laugh and she says it again, louder, with even more terrible enunciation. I look about to see if any of our fellow passengers hear, but they all have earplugs in, tuned in to something else.

I smile back at Mum. I wonder if I'd known her when she was my age, whether we'd have been friends.

I force school out of my head. All the girls I feel so separate from. I don't want to bring it with me. That's not what this trip is for.

"I can't believe we're flying!" I say. "I am *so* excited! We're above the clouds!"

"I was a child the last time I took a plane," Mum says dreamily. "We were going to Portugal. Me and your aunty Clem, and Granny and Grandpa. To a villa with a swimming pool on a clifftop. It was two years before the Climate Laws came in. It felt like heaven! I don't suppose we'll be swimming this time." She pretends to shiver.

I frown. "I thought there was a pool? The most northerly swimming pool in the world, you said." The most northerly pool in the most northerly town. The settlement also once boasted the most northerly school, before all the people left.

Mum nods. "Oh yes! I suppose we can use it. If there's…" Her voice trails off.

"Time," I finish for her. I can always see it in Mum's face when work takes over. A wrinkling by the sides of her eyes; furrows deepening on her forehead.

"Well, you might not have time, but I will," I vow petulantly, not caring how I sound. Not here on a plane that's filled with grey middle-aged people, most of them barely bothered about the fact we're flying. How can they not be gazing out of the window absorbing it all?

Aviation is meant to be for essential reasons only but some of the passengers look far too accustomed to it. They're working on laptops, drinks on their tables clacking gently with ice. Some of them even have their eyes shut, sneaking in a quick snooze. What a waste!

Standards get eroded over time. That's why Mum says the Svalbard Rare Earths Project is important. People only put up with so many restrictions, and for so long, and then they want life to advance again. Greenlight is one of the companies promising that can happen. They're at the helm of the green economy.

Dad would say that's dangerous propaganda and we should all be learning to live with less. And I'm in the middle. No one cares what I think, and I'm not sure what's true anyway. What matters most is that I persuaded Mum to let me take a six-week break from school, and Mum persuaded Greenlight to let me go with her. It's going to be the trip of a lifetime!

I hold my yellow camera up to the window and click. A few seconds later, a black square of recycled film is fed out into the air. I waft it gently between my finger and thumb as a little box of clouds appears. I'm going to stick it on the first page of my travel journal. I want to remember this feeling forever. We're flying!

# Airport

Tromsø airport is full of hot circulated air that makes me think of a hospital waiting room. A strange, stuffy space where no one stays very long – just passengers passing time before their next flight.

Except the staff in the coffee shop. I watch the woman serving. She's young – she must only be a few years older than me, but she's clearly out the other side of school. Independent, free, and glamorous in that way some people are without even trying.

As if she can sense me watching her, she catches my eye and beckons me over. I look around, in case her signal was actually meant for someone sitting behind me. Someone older and more worthy of attention. But there isn't anyone, so I get up, propelled towards her.

Mum's got her nose in some papers. "Don't go out of

sight, Rory. They'll be calling our flight soon." She purses her lips, puzzling over an anomaly in the geological survey she's reviewing. She's stressed about assumptions in the original site report for the island. Some other geologist wrote it, but it's going to be Mum's job to present an updated version to the Arctic Council when they make their final environmental assessment for the mine. I leave her lost in details about depths and seams and lengths of pipeline.

"You're young, for a flight," the coffee shop attendant says when I reach the counter.

"Yes, yes," I say, stumbling over my feet slightly. The woman's even prettier close up. She smells of petals, and I get this flashback to our old garden. Making perfume in the summer from fallen rose petals. Betty and I dabbing it on our necks. It smelled like ice cream. "I came from the UK. We're waiting for a flight to Longyearbyen."

"Longyearbyen? In Svalbard?" The woman's voice rises in surprise.

"Yes. Then we're getting a boat north to Pyramiden, the mining town," I say, faster now, squeezing my fists together in excitement. "We're with Greenlight. Well, my mum is. She's working on the Svalbard project."

The woman raises her eyebrows but keeps on smiling. "This time of year? I hope you've got enough layers to put on!"

"I have. Got warm things, I mean. We ordered them especially." My suitcase is full of thick waterproof trousers, a weatherproof jacket like a quilt and the puffiest boots I ever saw. Snow boots. For real snow!

"Would you like a drink?" the woman offers. "On me. Or on my boss, rather!" She winks mischievously and checks over her shoulder, but the little kitchen area behind her is empty. I look down at the metallic counter with a meagre selection of sandwiches in paper bags and bottles of fruit juice with flavours I can't decipher. "Take your pick. I don't normally get to serve anyone under forty," she says. "You're refreshing for me."

I like her choice of words, and the way she pronounces them in her Norwegian accent. I read her name badge. Nora.

"I'd like a tea, please," I say, trying to sound grown up.

Nora laughs, like I deliberately cracked a joke. "So English! Tea, please!" Then her smile becomes fiercer as she starts making the drink. "Lucky English girl, taking her first flight."

"Have you been up there?" I turn my head to the vaulted glass ceiling through which I can see grey sky.

"Of course not!" Nora laughs, brushing her hair back. "I'm a waitress in a coffee shop. I would never be permitted. You must be more important than me."

She doesn't look resentful or angry, but the words linger

in the recycled airport air.

"It's my mum that's important," I say. "At least her job is. She's going to check the site and advise on all kinds of things." I wave my hand vaguely. I don't ever really know much of what Mum's job involves, just that she's contracted as new buildings are planned, to make site maps and advise the engineers on ground conditions. This will be the first time she's worked for a mining company, but apparently she did a whole thesis on permafrost at university so she's a great fit for the Arctic.

"Ah, your mother is a scientist," Nora declares, pushing a cup across the counter to me.

"An environmental geologist," I correct.

"Ah!" Nora says again, no less certainly. "She found the metals. These precious metals that will allow us to take flights and live in luxury again."

There's a strange tone to her voice. Not like the girls at school, when they throw jokes back and forth and ignore any attempts I make to join in. This is more a general disbelief that the world will ever be any different than it is now.

I shake my head, anxious to avoid misunderstandings. "Mum's not been to Svalbard before. She's just supervising the last stage of the environmental assessment. She's taken me out of school, so I can be with her."

I can't resist getting that in. Nora must see the significance of this. It can't have been long ago that she'd have been at school too, in a stiff-shouldered blazer. Like a hamster in a wheel, ever turning, only I'm getting to spring off for a while.

"Nora!" A cross voice sounds behind her, followed by words I don't understand but I can tell the meaning of at once. Nora shouldn't be talking to me. I'm not important enough and there are tables to be cleared. A man appears, his face red and bad-tempered.

Nora turns to the sink to wring out a cloth. "Good luck, English girl," she says over her shoulder. "Watch out for the bears!"

Dirty water drips from the grey cloth into the silver bowl.

"Thank you for the tea!" I answer quietly, retreating away from the man's glare.

I wander over to the window with my steaming mug of tea. The window's large and round, like a spoked wheel.

I'd hoped for snow this far north, but rain is falling on the tarmac outside.

*Rain is English like tea*, I think, except in summer when we go for weeks and weeks without any rain at all. When the hosepipe ban starts and the parks and road verges turn to straw, and the fire stations are put on alert for wildfires.

Mum comes to stand beside me to look out at the runway, with its white and red planes and its spaceship control tower.

"You got a drink?" she asks, surprised.

"You want some?" I say, offering it to her.

Mum shakes her head. "No, you enjoy it. I'd just be trailing to the loo! It's only ten minutes till boarding time – next stop Longyearbyen!"

There are hills in the distance, grey and rocky, with patches of orange moss and lichen. This is tundra – a landscape above the tree line. The only verticals visible on the slope are steadily turning wind turbines.

"Do you think it will be snowing when we get there?" I wonder out loud. The rain gleams on the tarmac like spilt oil.

"Some of the time," Mum replies. "Apparently it can get windy too. Sometimes the wind blows the snow away into the sea."

"I hope it's snowing," I say emphatically. "I want to walk through it and make footprints. Or snow angels!"

Mum smiles indulgently. "It did snow once. When you were a toddler. We took you to the park and you kept picking it up, until your fingers got too cold in your gloves and your toes in your wellington boots. We hadn't thought to put extra socks on. You howled! Your dad had to carry you home on his back!"

She's laughing.

I give an irritated grunt. "I didn't know then, did I? That that was the last time I would see snow for a decade."

I can't keep the irritation from my voice. Mum's told this story before and for some reason it always annoys me. My one experience of snow and I was too young to make the most of it or remember.

I stare out of the window imagining landing on Svalbard. The land of snow and ice, bears, reindeer and white foxes. It seems almost impossible that it still exists.

# Landing

I first spot the mountains topped in snow. Actual snow! Like icing sugar poured down from the stars. Or white cotton sheets, bleached in the sunlight.

A tingle runs through my shoulder blades.

"Look!" I whisper to Mum. "Look!" I can't keep the tremble from my voice.

Triangular rockfaces rise up from the navy water of the fjords that surround the island. We swoop downwards, our plane a giant bird. I hold my breath as we sink further, into a landscape of orange and yellow, spread flat under high mountains.

The grey face of one of the mountains appears ominously close through the plane's windows. Then a town, off to the left, and beneath us. It must be Longyearbyen. Our stopping point on Spitsbergen before we go by boat through the fjords up to Pyramiden tomorrow. There are rows of colourful wooden houses in red, orange, yellow, mint green and blue. They have steep pitched roofs so the snow falls off them more readily. There are less photogenic buildings too from past mining days – old lifting gear, a metal warehouse, cableways and cranes.

Some of the town is covered in snow but before I can look properly we're past it, flying over the runway, fast, faster. I feel a flood of terror, that we're going to sink into the dark water of the fjord ahead, but there's a jolt as we bump down on to the runway, and a low screech as the plane's brakes start to work.

Mum's hand settles over mine as the plane slows. I realize how tightly I'm gripping the arm rest. My knuckles are hard as stone.

"Deep breaths, Rory!" Mum says, laughing gently. "We're on solid ground again."

"Has there been an avalanche?" I ask, pointing through the window to an assortment of buildings, half buried in snow, at the bottom of the mountain.

"The parts of the town still occupied have snow fencing to protect them," Mum says, not quite answering my question. "Those buildings over there won't be used any more. There are barely any people left here in the archipelago. Just a few climate scientists and university students, and of course people connected with Greenlight now, en route to the mine."

"And the mining town we're going to, Pyramiden, does that have snow fencing too?" I ask nervously. I've never thought about the power of snow before, to cover landscapes and buildings. Dad isn't here to carry me back now.

"Of course!" Mum says, squeezing my hand. "I wouldn't bring you here if it was unsafe. It's going to be basic, but not unsafe. Providing you stay in the defined parts of the town. Which you need to anyway because of the bears."

I nod, hugging my legs, allowing that tug of excitement to find its way back again. We've come to the far north. Whales, polar bears, reindeer, Arctic foxes, ptarmigans, ringed seals, walrus. I made a list on the plane of all the animals and birds that might still be here at this time of year. I'm going to take photos of everything. Not to mention the best light show on Earth – the *aurora borealis*.

It's going to be a true adventure, like in the books Dad read to me when I was small. Tales of forests and frozen lakes and more stars than you ever would have believed existed, burning in galaxies light years away. Here we're even further north than most of those stories.

I put my hand on the rounded square of window. I can feel the cold through the glass.

"Come on, Rory!" The seatbelt sign has flashed off and

Mum's opening the overhead locker to get down our hand luggage.

"We'll find the hotel and get checked in, and then we can go sightseeing! Greenlight have said they'll organize a guide for us."

I stand up, the thrill of excitement burning in my chest now.

Stepping from the plane on to the runway, the air hits my face in a rush, crisp and cold, and I breathe it into my lungs, to experience it all through my body.

"Are you ready, Rory? Our adventure begins!" Mum says beside me, bundled up in her new thick coat, her breath spiralling out into the clear air.

# Bear

Longyearbyen airport is smaller than Tromsø. It's barely as big as the bus station back home.

The man at passport control frowns when Mum says we are with Greenlight, and hands us both forms to complete.

I pause at the section 'Reason for essential travel' and tug Mum's arm to get her attention. She leans over and writes in capitals on the printed line: 'CHILD OF GREENLIGHT EMPLOYEE (LONE PARENT)'. I pull a face.

Mum had to apply for an exemption to allow me to accompany her. She pretty much declared Dad parentally unfit in the process.

Dad didn't object. He knew how badly I wanted not to go to school for a while. He'd seen me at my worst. The days I'd not made it into school and had bunked off to the forest instead, catching two buses there on my own.

Mum had been furious, with Dad more than me. She said he encouraged it, which wasn't fair.

I wish Dad could have come here with us. He's never taken a flight his whole life. His parents wouldn't have entertained the idea. They'd been living low impact lives years before the new laws made it compulsory.

The man peers at my form suspiciously, but it must pass whatever test it needs to because we're nodded through without a smile. I gasp as we turn a sharp corner into baggage reclaim. Above the turning conveyor of assorted luggage is the giant white form of a polar bear.

"It's stuffed!" I exclaim, caught between wonder and horror at the sight of the massive beast.

"Let's hope so," Mum says, walking up to it. "I suppose we have come to the home of the bears."

"Living ones!" I squeal. "I didn't think hunting was allowed."

"Relax, Rory." Mum laughs gently. "I'm sure this bear is much older than either of us. It's looking a bit mangy, like those foxes out by your dad's. Anyway, aren't you pleased? Polar bears were top of your list of animals to see, weren't they?"

"Mum!" I groan. "Taxidermy doesn't count."

"There are our suitcases, Rory! Quick!" Mum cries, running towards the conveyor. I help her heave our cases off the circular conveyor belt and on to a luggage trolley, which we wheel outside to find a taxi, the wheels skidding along the floor.

Out on the street, the snow has been scraped away and is piled up in slushy heaps. I glance at the people waiting in the queue ahead of us, wondering what they're doing here and what their essential reasons are. They look more like business people than climate scientists or naturalists and I feel a pang of disappointment.

Since the Global Climate Laws came in, there's been a rise in the numbers of animals in Svalbard. It's gradual, but it's happening. Like grizzly bears and Siberian tigers in the forests of Russia and Canada, and black rhinos and lions in Botswana's Okavango Delta. That's the point of the Wilderness Zones. And because these zones soak up carbon, they might save us too. If we leave them alone.

People are a slippery slope. If you say yes to one person, how can you say no to the next? And it doesn't take many people before a wilderness isn't really wild any more.

Mum and I stay glued to the car windows on the short drive into town. On one side is the sea, or the fjord rather – a deep narrow stretch of water reaching inland from the Greenland Sea. On the other side is a mountain. Both look as grey and stark as the other, and I'm glad when the cheery colours of the houses come into view, even if most of them look deserted.

We pull up on a long street with a few shops and

more boarded-up buildings. There's a neon hotel sign lit, however, making it clear where we're headed.

"Enjoy your trip," the taxi driver tells us neutrally. Mum opens her purse but the driver waves her hand dismissively. "It's on the Greenlight account."

In the hotel, Mum strides forwards to the reception desk to check us in. I can tell how excited she is about our time here, even if she has been muttering under her breath as she works through mistakes in the paperwork she's been given.

There's a bookcase in the reception area. 'Ice Library', a sign says over the top. I wander over. The books all have titles connected with the polar regions and I run my fingers over the spines greedily. I'm impatient to get into it for real now.

The young man on reception is asking about me and I kneel down beside the books, not wanting to listen.

I pick a book from the shelf. The cover shows a white lake surrounded by grey mountains, or perhaps it's a fjord like the ones we just flew over. I read the title under my breath. "*Dark Matter. A Ghost Story.*" There's a brown circle on the front where someone put down a mug of coffee.

Mum's hands on my shoulders make me jump. She's biting her lip.

"Was it OK?" I ask, a sudden sinking feeling in my stomach. "They're not going to send me back home?"

Mum looks surprised. "Send you back? Of course not. It's nothing about you." She runs her fingers through her hair. "There's a briefing I'm meant to attend in the hotel's conference room."

"Now?" I ask, pouting with annoyance. What about our plans to explore?

Mum sighs. "In fifteen minutes. It's with the Greenlight company director, Andrei. He's here in Longyearbyen meeting with investors. He wanted to catch me before we get the boat tomorrow. There was some background information I wasn't informed of…"

I raise my eyebrows questioningly.

"Settlers. Old mining families," Mum continues. "In Pyramiden."

"But it's a ghost town!" I retort.

Mum sinks down into one of the armchairs and makes a clucking sound at the front of her mouth. She's thinking. "Apparently some of the workers stayed after the last attempt to make the old mine operational. Properly stayed, as in had families here. *Children*." Her brow furrows extra deep as she says this last word.

"How do they survive there?" I ask, astonished at this new information. "What do they eat?"

"Reindeer. They've claimed subsistence hunting rights, just taking what they need to survive. And then they use whatever dried or canned food they manage to get their hands on, I imagine. It's totally against Wilderness Zone rules." Mum shakes her head. "No one even seems sure how many people there are, which is frustrating. The Arctic Council is meant to be on top of all this."

"Does it make any difference for Greenlight, though?" I ask. "Having people around?"

"This is a wilderness project, Rory. They picked the site precisely because there isn't anyone nearby." I try not to rise at the sarcasm in Mum's voice. She's always stressed at the beginning of a new contract, and this is the biggest job she's had in ages. Maybe ever.

I tilt my head. "They're going to need people to work in the mine. Couldn't they employ some of these settler people? Then they wouldn't need to bring over as many workers. Surely that would be better – fewer flights."

I expect Mum to agree with my suggestion but when she takes in what I've said she just purses her lips tighter. "Any miners from that time are probably too old to work now, and our methods are so different anyway. And any younger ones, well, what will they know about anything if they've lived their whole lives out here, closed off from the world?"

I stare back at her. It's not like Mum to dismiss people she hasn't met.

"Anyway, we'll make it work," she says with forced brightness. Her eyes go to the book in my hands. "A ghost story? I don't want you having nightmares!"

"It might be fun," I say defensively, but I put the book back on the shelf anyway. Nightmares are a sore point. I had so many after we left our old house and they only got worse after Dad moved out.

"Shall we go and see our room?" I say, trying to rescue the situation.

I'm excited about staying in a hotel, even if it is just for one night. It's been years since I went on a holiday. And since Betty moved away, I haven't even had a sleepover.

Mum looks back to a clock hanging over the reception desk. It's huge, with smaller clocks around it showing the time in New York, Tokyo, Moscow and Bangkok. Behind the desk, the man smiles over at us and points to our suitcases, abandoned in the middle of the lobby like little islands. "Your room's on the third floor. I can help with the cases if you like? They look heavy."

"Oh yes, please," Mum answers, standing up again. "That's kind of you. And is it OK for my daughter to wait here this afternoon? It sounds like I need to hurry to the meeting room for that briefing."

The man glances at me sympathetically. "Surely your daughter – Rory, isn't it? – would like to explore our town while the light lasts? There's less than an hour to go before sunset and you're only here one night."

"Yes, but..." Mum frowns. "That would be unsafe, wouldn't it, on her own? The bears?"

My heart drums in my chest. Yesterday I was in my humdrum town and now there's the prospect of running into a polar bear.

The man smiles. "You'll be fine in the town itself, Rory. We have trip wire warning systems and the boundary is well marked. Just don't go beyond there."

I nod excitedly back at him. He must see the hunger in me to explore.

"I'll be careful, Mum," I promise. "I really want to see the seed vault. To take a photo, for Dad."

The seed vault is dug into the mountainside above town, in case of further climate disaster or nuclear war or some other apocalyptic end. A million types of seeds, which could help people grow food crops if they needed to start from scratch. Dad and I found out about it on the computer in the town library. I clutch the camera strap around my neck, feeling sad for a moment, thinking of Dad out in the forest, watching the leaves change colour without me.

The man shakes his head. "I'm afraid the seed vault is too far out of town."

I look at Mum, hoping she'll have a suggestion. She'd been so sure about the guide Greenlight would provide for us in our short time here, but she only smiles vacantly. "Just walk up the main street then, Rory. Get a feel for the place. Buy some sweets or something, and take some pictures to show me over dinner. I promise you I'll make up for it then."

The man flicks me another sympathetic smile. I guess I'm exploring Longyearbyen alone.

# 78 Degrees North

The main street is mostly empty. The sun's already hidden behind the mountains and it's much colder than when we arrived. There's a scattering of frozen snow on the pavement.

'Dark days make for cold days', it says in my Arctic book.

I take a selfie outside the hotel sign. *Hotel Longyearbyen. 78 Degrees North.* If you looked at the globe in our geography classroom at school, I'd be almost at the top.

Longyearbyen started out as a mining town, making money from extracting coal, back in the days before people knew what that was doing to the planet. Or if they did know, they didn't care. Didn't care about the blackening air and the invisible gases collecting in the atmosphere, absorbing far more heat from the sun than our planet can stand.

'*Gjelder hele Svalbard*,' I read from another sign, this one with a white bear in a red warning triangle.

I imagine a bear like the one from baggage reclaim, lumbering down the street towards me. Or maybe it wouldn't lumber. Maybe it would be fast and precise, moving towards its target.

I type the Norwegian words into my phone for a translation. 'Applies to all of Svalbard.' I glance around nervously. As much as I want to see a polar bear, I'm not ready to meet a real-life one yet.

There's a small supermarket and I go in, because there's a grumbling in my stomach. I have a few notes which Mum thrust into my hand before she ran off for her meeting.

My nose twitches at the strong scent of fish in the shop, but I push on past jars of pickles and jams. The bright colours are appealing, even though I don't recognize all the things on the labels.

"Can I help you?" a woman asks in English over by the counter. "You're new here."

She looks at me strangely. I'm the only customer in the shop, I realize.

"I'm with Greenlight," I answer, a touch of pride in my voice.

The expression shifts on the woman's face. "More people already? But the Council's approval isn't granted yet?" She narrows her eyes at me.

"I came with my mum. She's a geologist."

The woman nods her head, but there's a sharpness in her now.

I step back and knock against one of the shelves. It rattles loudly.

"Oh, I'm sorry! I just came to buy sweets," I say, blushing and moving away from the shelf. I pick up the first confectionary item I see. A packet of chocolate hearts, filled with something that looks like caramel.

I pass one of the notes over the counter. "Is this enough?"

The shop lady nods silently, taking the note and counting out silver coins from the till. She places them on the countertop before me. They have holes like polo mints.

"Thank you," I say quietly, tucking the change into my pocket. I've never held foreign coins before but I'm not going to stop and look at them now. I'm desperate to get away from the woman's hostile stare.

The icy air hits me afresh going out. I wander a bit further up the street but the next two shops – both outdoor clothing places – look empty, and after that all the shops are boarded up.

It's darker now and even with the orange streetlights I'm nervous to go further from the hotel alone. I turn around, opening the chocolate for the way back.

The hearts are sweet and rich, and the caramel inside both sticky and dry at the same time. I wonder if they've been kept too long on that countertop. I zip them back into one of the pockets of my coat.

I start suddenly as I spy another stuffed polar bear in an empty shopfront opposite. I cross to have a better look. Small black eyes stare into the dim street. I meet their gaze. I remember that polar bears have transparent fur and it's just an optical trick that makes them appear white. This one just looks yellowy grey, and old and worn. Poor thing. I wonder when it last had blood coursing through it? Who thought it a good idea to put it here for everyone to see, like some weird art installation?

I walk past that sign again. *Gjelder hele Svalbard.* The man at the hotel said the main street was safe, but what's to stop a polar bear wandering down the street looking for dinner? What's a trip wire warning system anyway? A line of wire isn't going to stop a polar bear, is it? They're predators, right at the top of the food chain.

Hairs bristle on the back of my neck. The cold feels like it's entered my actual bones and I'm glad when I make it back to the hotel.

By the chairs in the lobby there's a fire now with crackling logs, which must have been brought in from a managed forest like Dad's. The smell is smoky and familiar.

I pick a high-backed chair facing away from the reception desk and flick through the books from the Ice Library. A nervousness has crept into my stomach, like a moth is trapped inside and fluttering to get out. I wish it would stop. I didn't want to be nervous here. I wanted to be brave and excited, like the old explorers must have been who first found this place.

I give the ghost story a miss and pick up a guide to the birds of Svalbard.

Most birds are summer visitors only, I read, migrating here in the warmer months to catch fish and crustaceans. They make their nests on rocky cliff faces where they're safe from predators.

They leave as it gets colder. Only the ptarmigan stays all year round, a plump bird that turns white in winter. I know lots of this already from the book Dad gave me.

I start skimming through a history book, about the animal trappers and hunters of Svalbard. It has pictures of wooden huts on desolate beaches that look as remote as the moon. I remember how back in primary school we learned that the Arctic is actually a desert because of lack of rain but that Climate Change might alter that – we don't know what warming trajectory we're still on.

I consciously push that thought away. I don't want to think about this place melting.

There are interesting captions under the hut photos. I read about an Austrian woman who spent a whole winter on a remote part of the island called Gray Hook, with her hunter-trapper husband, over 130 years ago.

"Rory, you're back." Mum appears above me and flops down into the chair opposite. I can predict what's coming from her expression.

"You can't do dinner, can you?" I say, my eyes burning. It's not just dinner, it's our one night in this place, probably ever.

"Of course I can," Mum says, though the way the words form on her lips makes me wonder if she's this second adjusted what she was going to say. "We'll have dinner. It's just we're going to have company."

"What do you mean 'company'?" I ask suspiciously.

"Andrei wants me to meet the investors. They're flying back to Norway first thing tomorrow. He has a table booked at the town's restaurant. Perhaps you can bring that book." She glances down at it. "It looks interesting."

"But it's our first night, and our only night here, and..." I falter, leaving the rest unsaid. I want to show Mum the polar bear and how your breath forms clouds in the cold air. I want us to look up at the grey mountains together and her to find that guide we'd been promised to show us the seed vault above the town. Its entranceway is meant to light up like a thousand stars.

"I know, sweetheart, but you can see the position I'm in. This is the company director asking. It's crucial for the whole project that we get the investors' backing."

I clench my fingers into a ball. None of my needs seem

important when you compare them to Mum's work. Global green energy has a habit of making everything else seem insignificant. What can one child matter in the face of worldwide catastrophe?

"Sure," I say, breathing out loudly. "What time? I'll go and get ready."

"Sorry, Rory," Mum says, putting her hand on my shoulder as I get up and giving me another squeeze. "I'll see you at 7 p.m. here in the lobby. Make sure you bring your new coat. It's only a couple of minutes away, but the temperature out there is plummeting."

# Restaurant

The restaurant is warm and bright, in pointed contrast to the frozen street outside. Wooden picnic bench style tables are laid out in a row, and covered in a cheery red cloth, below low hanging lights.

After taking off my boots at the door and putting them inside a set of cubbyholes, I grab a seat at the end of one of the benches, between the window and a row of hanging coats. As out of view as I can get.

It's nighttime already here, or a strange kind of twilight because the streets still have their snow glow, reflecting back the moonlight.

Mum didn't even glance at the sky on her way over. She was head down, following her new boss, Andrei, who she hasn't even bothered introducing me to. I'd fallen silently behind.

Dad would have looked. He'd have stopped dead in his tracks and stood and stared till his feet froze on the pavement. The stars here are piercing.

I scrutinize the menu. It's in English, but that doesn't help. All the options seem to involve fish or meat. 'Reindeer meat', I read. Is this for real?

Mum catches me frowning. "The Arctic Council sees them as sustainable options out here. It makes sense. It's not like at home."

"But what do *we* eat?" I whisper. At home, we're permitted fish or meat three times a week but I've never bothered. Just because you can do something doesn't mean you should. Mum doesn't normally eat any of those things either.

"Are you sure you don't want to try the salmon? It's a good opportunity, and oily fish in these conditions might be good for you," Mum tries, ignoring my indignant face. "You have to adapt according to your environment."

One of the youngest members of the group, who's sat opposite us, leans across the table. "You're vegetarian, Rory?"

I nod happily, pleased she's learned my name.

She winks. "Order the *lefse* then. It's a type of flatbread, made from potatoes. You can order it with cheese and vegetables, like a kind of pizza. It's good, I promise. That's what I'll have." She rubs her stomach happily.

"I'm Katerina. I can order for us both."

I smile gratefully. "Oh, yes, please."

"This must be quite a trip for you," Katerina says. "You're the youngest person I've seen in Longyearbyen!"

"Rory's my keen assistant," Mum says, putting her arm round me.

"Mum." I squirm. "Are you with Greenlight too?" I ask Katerina. She doesn't look like the rest of the people round the table. She's so much younger for a start and seems slightly detached from their conversations.

"Not me," she answers lightly. "I'm at Oslo university, in my final year. There's a small polar studies department based out here. We're interested in the Rare Earths Project."

There's a weight to the word 'interested' but Katerina seems friendly enough with everyone in the restaurant. Though I've noticed her give Mum's boss Andrei some strange glances when he becomes particularly loud and assertive about Greenlight's unblemished environmental record.

On my side of the table are three Greenlight employees: two men and a woman, and then Mum, next to me, who I guess is one of them now. Directly opposite are – I soon realize – the investors. With Andrei at the head of the table, like he's holding court.

"They just got back from Pyramiden." Katerina speaks in a hushed tone, clocking my glance at the investors.

"I don't think it was quite as they expected."

"Have you been there?" I ask her, keen to get a first-hand report of our base for the next few weeks.

Katerina nods. "I went in the summer, soon after I arrived on the island."

"Did you meet the old miners?" I probe. "What are they like?"

Katerina nods again, thoughtful now. "I don't think they liked so many newcomers. Big machinery was being brought in. Greenlight was starting initial excavations… It's a lot of disruption if that's your home. They were worried it would upset the reindeer. The community there has become very reliant on those creatures!" She smiles again and looks at my travel journal open on the table.

"I was just making a few notes, about our flight, and today," I explain shyly.

"I keep a journal too," Katerina tells me comfortably. "It won't last forever, this place. Even with the Global Climate Laws, the ice is still melting. It's good to keep a record of it."

"Yes," I say earnestly. "That's it! I know how lucky I am."

Katerina is drawn into the conversation about mining and I go back to doodling the shape of the archipelago as it appeared below us from the plane window, and dreaming about the Svalbard reindeer. It sounds like we should see lots of them.

I don't even try to keep up with everything they're saying

around the table. The investors seem to have a lot of questions.

When the *lefse* arrives it's tasty and filling. Katerina smiles when she sees my empty plate. "It's good, huh?" But she quickly turns back to the adults. She asks questions that get the investors looking nervous and Andrei looking angry. About how they plan to deal with waste products, and how water is involved in the process and what's going to be the difference in winter when all the water's frozen.

I look out of the restaurant window. The mountains are blue now, looming over the town. I remember the snow-covered buildings we saw from the runway and wonder how many avalanches this town has seen.

Andrei's talking loudly about Greenlight's 'revolutionary' refining techniques. They're using a bacteria to get the rare earth elements out of the rock and he claims this will leave no trace on the landscape. That doesn't fit with what Katerina told me about the big machines and the excavations but I know I haven't been listening carefully enough to follow everything.

I begin writing notes in my journal, around the doodles. That rush of adrenaline as the plane took off. The bird's eye view of my hometown – my school almost beautiful from so far away – then the sea, and new lands appearing beneath us. Nora in the café at Tromsø airport. I draw the shelves of the Ice Library and scribble down the titles I can remember. *Dark Matter. A Woman in the Polar Night. Arctic Dreams.*

I wish it could just be Mum and me, at a little table in the corner, snug under the beamed ceiling. Some of the voices are tense, and they get more urgent the more wine everyone drinks. The investors are not so bothered by Katerina's questions about waste and chemicals, but they keep pressing Mum on the "longevity" of the mine. They're worried they won't make "sufficient profit" if the "deposits" aren't rich enough. I don't think they know Mum hasn't even visited the mine yet.

Mum's polite and open but I can tell she's on edge. I feel sorry for her. Ever since she found out she was coming, she's had her head in the paperwork. She says it's no better than guesswork in places. But she's obviously been told to give only the positives today, and if she even pauses, Andrei comes in with a sweeping statement about how great and successful they're sure it's all going to be.

I stifle a yawn and Mum turns to me sympathetically. "Shall I walk you back to the hotel, Rory?"

Katerina turns back to us. "Listen, I'm done in. I can take Rory back. You stay and answer their questions, Laura."

"Are you sure? I don't want to put you to any trouble," Mum says, glancing awkwardly back at her new colleagues. Andrei is looking disdainfully down the table.

"Honestly, it's no trouble. I've heard enough," Katerina

assures us, getting to her feet and claiming her coat from the hooks by the door. "I'm heading back to my dorm. I can drop Rory at the hotel on the way."

Mum looks at me for guidance, thinking I'll be too shy to go off with a stranger. But I'm longing to get into the clean white sheets of my hotel room and I don't want to get Mum in trouble with Andrei.

"Great," I say to Katerina, putting my journal back into my rucksack.

The cold on the street shocks me.

"Are you OK, Rory?" Katerina says, sensing me tense up.

"I'm still getting used to it," I answer through clenched teeth.

"I'd like to say you do get used to it." Katerina smiles. "But I think you just learn to wear more clothes."

I pull my bobble hat further down over my ears.

There's a light sprinkling of snow on the ground that wasn't there earlier. How did I not notice it fall? It's freezing already in a delicate pattern, caught in the light from the restaurant window. "Can you wait a second?" I say shyly to Katerina, struggling with numb fingers to get out my phone. Even though I'm shivering, I can't resist crouching down to take a photo of the swirls of frost.

"Of course," Katerina says warmly. "You should see how many photos I took in the beginning!"

I almost slip as I stand and Katerina links arms with me

for support. "I don't want you sliding into the gutter on your first night!"

We come to a bar just before the hotel. The windows are fogged with condensation and you can hear the noise through the glass. Music, conversation, laughter. It seems strange to have a noisy gathering in such a remote place.

"That looks more fun than the Greenlight investors' dinner, huh?" Katerina says, winking at me.

I laugh.

"It gets rowdy at this time of year," she continues. "People have their last parties before the winter."

"What happens in winter?" I ask curiously.

Katerina shrugs. "Oh, most people leave. Some stay but they have to hibernate. Slow down. Sleep!"

We're back at the hotel now. The lights in the lobby are on and there's a different person behind the desk.

"Are you OK finding your way in, Rory?" Katerina checks.

I nod firmly. "Thank you for walking me back."

"No worries, Rory. It was a pleasure. And good luck in Pyramiden. Take plenty of photos!"

I watch her make her way back into the muted artificial light of the street.

She said she was tired, but she turns into that bar we passed, to join the party. Maybe it was Andrei and the investors she'd had enough of.

# Leviathan

Mum hurries us along to Longyearbyen harbour, dragging her suitcase along the uneven road surface. I struggle behind with my smaller one. It's barely light – the sky is violet and pink, with an eerie yellow light emanating from the horizon.

"You could have let me finish my breakfast," I grumble, wiping sleep from my eyes. The hotel had served waffles and I could happily have eaten half a dozen. They were laden with the most delicious jam I'd ever tasted. Made from cloudberries, the waiter said. It was ruby red and tasted of forests and flowers, but I'd only managed a couple of waffles before Mum ordered me up to my room to pack.

Mum turns back to me. "Oh, Rory! I'm sorry! You have to make the most of the daylight here. Andrei scheduled departure at first light."

We're walking over with one of the Greenlight people from yesterday. Mark, he's called, and he seems to be Andrei's assistant or something. He has a gun slung over his shoulder, which makes me uneasy, even though I know it's for our protection.

There's no mistaking which boat we're taking. It's the only one in the harbour that looks watertight. The rest could be in a ship graveyard. Some containers are stacked ready for loading by a small pier and we leave our suitcases next to them.

There's no sign of Andrei or any of the others yet.

Mark shrugs. "They'll be here soon. Andrei runs on his own time." He wanders down the waterfront whistling.

Mum and I stroll to the edge of the water where there are large ducks bobbing and diving down for food.

"Eider ducks, look," I say, perking up a bit and taking photos with my phone. "Sea ducks!" They're so perfectly like the ones in that book yesterday. The females are brown, the males black and white with a green tinge on their necks like spring leaves.

Mum pushes me affectionately. "See, something to tick off your list! I wonder what else we'll see on the crossing. It's meant to take a good few hours."

Pyramiden is on the same island as Longyearbyen, but you get there through the fjords. There are no big roads like there are back home.

Across the water are mountains with snow-covered tops. They're mirrored in the fjord, amidst curls of cloud.

Mum and I studied the maps together at home excitedly, but it was hard to imagine it. And now we're standing here, watching eider ducks swim on an Arctic fjord, snow-covered mountains all around. I can't quite believe it.

"I wonder where the others are?" Mum says. "The captain was meant to be here already." She looks over at Mark, who's staring into the water pensively, clearly not bothered about making conversation with us.

Before I can say anything, there's a burst of voices.

Mum stands to attention as Andrei comes down the road from the main town, with a couple of the other Greenlight employees from last night. Mark walks to meet them and is handed Andrei's bag to carry.

I linger by the waterside, holding my phone camera up to get a shot of the boat. *Leviathan*, I read on the hull. I recognize the word from my Arctic book. It means sea monster, but whalers and explorers used it to describe the great whales they caught in these waters. The fjords and seas were teeming with them when people first came here, seals and walrus too.

The *Leviathan* couldn't have been a whaling boat, could it? Even though it looks ancient, it's not *that* ancient,

I decide. Still, the thought of travelling north in it makes me shiver.

I try to shrug off the feeling of trepidation that's settling on my shoulders. This is an adventure!

My thoughts are interrupted by a man jumping down from the boat on to the harbour side, clearing his throat gruffly. He's dressed in a thick jumper and red hat, but other than that, it's like he's not bothered by the cold.

Andrei moves forwards to meet him, tapping his watch. "Our captain," he says, his voice laden with sarcasm. "Only half an hour late."

I look at Andrei in surprise. He's only just arrived himself!

"You should start loading up, if you want to get those things to Pyramiden," the captain says curtly, pointing out the containers.

"Isn't that what we're paying you for, to get things there?" Andrei says, smiling the kind of smile that only involves teeth and lips. "And back again."

"I'm paid to steer my ship," the captain answers disdainfully.

He moves deliberately away from Andrei, who instead orders Mark and the others to start loading up. Mum goes to check our suitcases make it on board, and the captain busies himself laying a small wooden bridge across from the dockside to the boat. I take a final few photos looking back towards the town and the strange mix of colours in the sky.

"Welcome aboard," the captain says when it's my turn to board over the rickety gangway. His eyes are grey, like steel.

I smile shyly, mesmerized by him. He looks like a character from an old storybook.

Andrei and Mark head straight down the steps into the bottom part of the boat. The captain watches them go, then adjusts his hat and breathes out sharply like he's tasted something disagreeable. I'm glad Andrei's gone too. I don't like the way he's taken to ordering Mum around, and the smarmy way he answered the investors' questions last night.

Mum and I stay sitting on the deck.

"Brace yourself!" the captain tells us, throwing a couple of orange life jackets our way. "The first part of the voyage can be choppy. Once we get into the open, the wind can rip this water apart."

"I'm sure we'll be OK," Mum says lightly, but I notice she takes care to ensure the straps on my life jacket are well fastened.

The *Leviathan* creaks and rocks as we unmoor and I take a deep breath and a sip of water from my bottle, steeling myself for the journey ahead. Choppy waters they might be, but I'm determined not to miss a thing.

# Fjords

The warehouses and colourful houses of Longyearbyen are soon behind us. We cut through the dark water of the fjord, the clouds low beside us now, damp and mysterious. An occasional gull soars overhead, following in the wake of the metal boat.

"Do you think the clouds will clear?" I whisper to Mum. I'm trying to scan the mountains on either side through breaks in the cloud. Looking for polar bears on the jagged peaks that rise up from the water.

"Let's hope the wind's in our favour," Mum says.

A couple of other Greenlight employees are up on the deck and Mum introduces them to me as mine operatives.

"You're missing your friends at school?" one of them asks.

I shake my head fiercely. It's a Tuesday morning, and

back home I'd only be a fraction through the week, wondering where to go at lunchtime and who I might sit with in the canteen. Wishing for the hundredth time that Betty had never moved away and that the cliques of girls at school didn't seem so impenetrable.

Mum eyes me sadly but I don't say anything. I'm not thinking about any of that, I'm concentrating on the here and now.

The man who addressed me points his finger ahead. "The clouds, they clear for you," he says, and I gaze to where he's pointing.

There's ice in the water. A frozen realm is appearing through the cloud, stark and beautiful. More snow caps on the chiselled mountains, sometimes reaching all the way down to the water, and remote grey shores you could only ever reach by boat. I spy a hut like the ones in the book yesterday.

Mum exhales beside me. "It's like a painting, isn't it? It doesn't seem real."

"How can Andrei and Mark still be below deck?" I say. They're like the people snoozing on the plane. I could never get bored of views like this.

We sail on into the icy water and I pull my gloves off, to take photos on my phone camera, even though my fingers tingle in complaint at the cold.

There's a sudden loud *plop*, and as I look over the side of the boat I spot a round grey head peering out of the water at us with dark shining eyes.

"Seals!" Mum and I gasp together. The more we look the more we see, on floating bits of ice, looking our way, ready to slip into the water with a splash if we get too close.

"It feels like we've sailed to the edge of the world," I whisper to no one in particular.

"You're glad you came then?" Mum smiles, laughing at my open-mouthed wonder. The world here clearly doesn't belong to people, it belongs to them – the seals and the gulls and whatever else is in these waters. My brain is slightly fuzzy that I'm here at all.

"Walrus!" I shout, rising on to my tiptoes. Three large mammals with elephant-like tusks are lolling together on a piece of floating ice.

I gaze at the browny-pink faces and their small eyes look back at me above bristly whiskered moustaches. I've seen footage of walrus in wildlife documentaries but seeing them so close is different. Their size, their sheer weight. One of them decides the sea is a safer option, and lumbers on its four flippers for a few seconds before disappearing into the water with a slap.

I hang over the edge of the boat to watch them glide past. The captain gives an amused smile. "They're more graceful than you think!" he says, just as the remaining walrus make deep-throated groans.

"In the water anyway," the captain adds, and Mum and I both laugh.

"You don't have many days of light left." The captain indicates the dusty glow of sun on the horizon. "She's sinking. *Polarnatt.*"

"*Polarnatt.*" I repeat the Norwegian word under my breath. The polar night. In the summer you get the midnight sun here – twenty-four hours of daylight – but in winter it's the opposite.

"We call this the blue season," the captain tells us.

Mum and I gaze at the haze of colours. Blue season. I take a photo with the yellow Polaroid, and one of the seals and walrus too.

"There was a whale earlier," the captain offers casually, like he's talking about a rat or a pigeon. "If you're interested in that kind of thing."

*If* I'm interested? Is my excitement not obvious?! It feels like all my senses have come alive out here.

I peer over the edge of the boat, scrutinizing the surface of the fjord.

"It was a bowhead," the captain continues. "She'll be coming up for air soon."

"A bowhead!" I squeal. I'm hoping to see a beluga and a narwhal too, but it's the bowheads I'm most intrigued by. They're a type of baleen whale and one of the biggest whales alive. Only the blue and fin whale would grow bigger.

Mum tenses, her hand on my shoulder. "Is it safe?"

The captain scoffs. "The baleens are gentle giants. They've a lot more to fear from you."

Mum smiles uneasily. She understands from the way he looks at her that it's not just a turn of phrase. He's having a dig at Greenlight.

"Greenlight's respect for the wilderness is at the heart of all its operations," Mum says, in a friendly way. Still, my stomach twists a little.

The captain doesn't say anything. He sucks in the cold air and readjusts his woolly hat.

"How long can they stay down for?" I can't resist asking after a while hanging over the edge and seeing nothing but water and ice.

"The bowhead?" the captain answers. "She can stay down an hour if she likes. Or she might have moved on now."

"Oh," I say, disappointed.

"Rory's desperate to see a whale," Mum comments. "She's been researching them for our trip."

"What did you find out about the bowhead?" the captain asks, as if to test me.

"I read that they're the longest-living mammal on Earth," I tell him, my voice clear and confident. "People have found stone harpoon heads in their blubber from a hundred and fifty years ago. And you can date the whales from their eyes too, after they've died. They have rings in them like trees."

The captain smiles, his head to one side listening.

"Do you know about Greenland sharks?" I can't resist asking. The captain seems like he might know all the sea's mysteries.

"Tell me about them," he says, a twinkle in his eyes.

"I read that they can be four hundred years old!"

My brain can't even comprehend that amount of time. It seems a miracle that something born so long ago could still be gliding through the seas, slow and quiet, hidden away from the world.

"And that they like the coldest part of the water," I add.

"I've seen a shadowy form once or twice next to the boat," the captain tells me. "Coming up to see how the world's changing. I don't know what they'd make of the mining starting up again."

He directs another accusatory look at Mum.

"Do you know," Mum says, her voice clear in the cold air, "there are untapped gas and oil reserves in the Barents and the Kara Sea? Some of the proposals put forward to the Arctic Council were to start deep-sea drilling, to bring it out. To burn it. Even though the world vowed never to burn fossil fuels again. When money gets involved, people will do anything."

The captain doesn't say anything. His eyes don't stray

from the dark water and the floes of ice like sculpted flowers. The further north we get, the more ice there is.

"I'm just saying," Mum continues, quietly now, but no less intently. "There were far worse options the Arctic Council could have backed than the Svalbard Rare Earths Project. This is a chance for this region to not just be a passive victim of climate change, but to be part of the solution. Of the new global green economy."

Mum's gone too far now in her sales pitch. Even I can see that the global green economy means nothing out here.

The *Leviathan* captain turns his head to me. "So anyway, it's the bowhead you want to watch for. Look out for her blows."

"They have two blow holes, don't they, the bowheads?" I say awkwardly, caught between loyalty to my mum and a desire to impress the captain.

Mum gives me a strange sideways glance. Maybe she's surprised at my confidence. I can't explain how different I feel already being here in the vastness of this new landscape. Everything is so raw and alive, it makes the blood run faster in my veins.

The captain is nodding at me, impressed. "You could come back and study them when you're old enough. Maybe my *Leviathan* will still be sailing these parts." He pats the wooden wheel in his hand affectionately.

Mum's still staring at me and I have this odd sensation,

like I'm floating away from her. A sudden smile stretches across her face. "Let me take a photo of you, Rory. Your dad would love to see you in the land of seals and walrus."

I shake my head. "It should be both of us together. We can take a selfie."

We lean in, our two smiling faces, the water, ice and rock of the archipelago behind us, terrifying and beautiful at the same time.

# Ghost Town

Pyramiden appears on the horizon like a mirage. A grid of utilitarian buildings built from brick in a barren wilderness, at the bottom of a severe grey mountain.

Everyone's up on the deck now, staring sombrely at the town. Even Andrei and Mark.

"Don't forget to eat your vitamins. You don't want to get scurvy." The captain issues last words of advice as I get ready to disembark.

I smile, unsure if he's making a joke, though Mum had sourced booster packs of vitamins for us both, with extra vitamin D because of the lack of sunlight. Vitamin D for strong bones and teeth.

"Thank you for bringing us over. It was amazing," I say, wishing I could find more profound words for the boat trip.

The captain nods impassively. "Keep watching for the whales." He turns away. There are metal containers on the dockside that are waiting to be lifted up on to the ship. He didn't want any part of the loading process in Longyearbyen, but now he starts directing what goes where, as though he wants it done as soon as possible.

Mum and I step across the *Leviathan*'s gangway towards a wooden walkway built over the grey-black shingle. My legs are shaky as they adjust to being on solid ground, even though it doesn't feel quite solid. The pathway threads through high, creaking metal structures on its way into town. It must be equipment from when the coal mine was working. All the coal would have had to come here, so it could be taken away by ship to be burned in some power station somewhere.

A young woman appears ahead of us, bundled up in cold weather gear. She's walking towards us with a rifle over her shoulder. *Gjelder hele Svalbard,* I remember.

"Welcome to Pyramiden," she calls cheerily. "I'm Pia. I'm a glaciologist on the project and unofficial welcomer today." Pink blooms spread over her cheeks under a turquoise bobble hat. I immediately decide I like her. "How was the *Leviathan*?"

"It was quite something," Mum says. "We've certainly never taken a trip like that before, have we Rory?"

I nod enthusiastically beside her.

"I'm so pleased to meet you, Pia," Mum gushes. "I've been reading some of your papers. It's going to be an honour to work with you here."

Pia puts up her hand dismissively. "Any glaciologist would have taken this project. It's rare for us to see glaciers in person! It's my privilege."

The buildings come into focus as we approach the town, in faded reds and browns. It's very different to the colourful palette of Longyearbyen. The buildings stand on concrete legs, like they don't quite trust the ground, and there are dark cavities beneath them.

A gull flutters out of one of the windows above and across a grassy square, half covered in snow, where a stone statue stands and stares through the old buildings. I feel a quiver of excitement at the thought of exploring this place.

Pia points back to the fjord to an edge of blue over the water. "Look at the glacier, see? That was what called me here."

Mum nods. "I was hoping we might get a chance to visit it."

"Oh yes, you must," Pia responds at once. "I insist! And that I come with you. I'll show you it."

I meet Mum's eyes greedily. "Can we?" I ask. "I'd love to get close to it."

"We can do better than that. We can get you *on* it, if we get some ice soles on your boots," Pia says. "We'll set a date, before the fjord freezes over too much, yes?"

I nod enthusiastically.

"Most of the buildings have fallen into disuse," Pia says, her eyes back on the square. "The children here play in them, but they're not used for any practical purpose."

"Ah, the children," Mum says. "I was just hearing about them. I didn't know."

Pia purses her lips. "Andrei has a habit of leaving that part out."

A horn blows from the waterside as the *Leviathan* starts its journey south.

"Sounds are strange here," Pia murmurs, looking back towards the water. "The air is so clear. Noises from far away seem much closer sometimes."

"Which building is the hotel?" Mum asks, laying her suitcase on the icy wood.

Pia's face falls. "Over there, you see the tallest building?"

It's easy to spot – it's by far the newest building, even though it's still old. It's four stories tall and looks reassuringly solid, with curved corners.

"The thing is, we've only managed to take over a small section of it," Pia continues. "The settler families have been using it, understandably, I suppose since it's the most modern building…"

Mum's frowning, knowing this is going somewhere she won't like.

Pia smiles thinly. "But we're renovating one of the other buildings as sleeping quarters. It's Building Nine on the plan you've been given." She points to one of the older buildings. It's murky white and there are bird nests in the window alcoves.

"That one?" Mum says, not managing to hide her disappointment.

Pia nods. "It's one of the old dormitory blocks. It's where the miners will go eventually, but you've both been put there for now." Pia runs her fingers through her long hair. "Some of the rooms still need a refit – yours, Rory, is one of the older ones I'm sorry to say. We hadn't got the message you were coming till quite late, but we obviously wanted you to be near your mum. You're across the corridor from each other."

"It doesn't matter," I say quickly, not minding that my room is old. Old feels right in this place. "I don't want to be any trouble."

"Not at all," Pia says. "It's nice to have another young person. Perhaps you'll make friends with the town children. We could do with a few more allegiances around here."

I push away the feeling of apprehension that's crept into my insides at the mention of the children. Maybe I can make friends out here.

Mum's jumped down from the wooden walkway to pick up a couple of rocks, switching into geology mode.

"Pia, Pia," sings a voice. A small head appears around the side of the nearest building – a tiny girl, with tousled brown hair arranged into plaits and fierce eyes.

"Marnie," Pia says affectionately. "We have guests. Look, this is Rory."

The little girl, Marnie, steps out on the square. She's followed by a succession of other children, aged from about five to around my age, who are making no attempt not to stare at me. I feel myself shrinking back, wishing myself invisible.

"How many children are here?" Mum asks, jolted back into the moment by their appearance.

Pia smiles vaguely. "A dozen or so. There's quite a resistance to us, in the town community. I'm sure you've been briefed…" Pia's voice tails off, and she looks back along the line of the walkway where Andrei's approaching now from the harbour, barking instructions to Mark as he walks. Pia turns her back on him, smiling at me now. "The young children are curious, of course. I'm sure you'll get on!"

The children don't look that friendly. They're talking behind their hands, in harsh whispers.

"Do they speak English?" Mum asks.

Pia nods. "It's the common language. The mining firm employed a range of different nationalities. Mostly people who'd been displaced after the Climate Laws."

"And what about education?" Mum goes on.

"Mum!" I groan, sinking into my boots, wishing she'd stop. The children have backed away, but I can tell they're listening. Especially the older ones.

Pia smiles neutrally. "It's different here. Things are different. Priorities, ambitions."

"The poor things will have been bored out of their wits," Andrei says loudly, coming up behind us. "It contravenes all kinds of rules."

A shadow crosses over Pia's face. She bites her lip.

Mum looks between her and Andrei uneasily.

"Has Pia told you where you're staying? We hadn't expected your child too." He tuts under his breath and I sink further into my boots. It's the first time he's acknowledged my existence.

"Rory and I come as a package," Mum says, pulling me into her warmly.

Andrei goes on undeterred. "Ridiculously we can't seem to accommodate all our employees in the hotel. Even though those people have no right to be living there."

"It was hardly running as a hotel, they might as well be," Pia says defensively. "Any of us would have done the same." She sighs pointedly, and then catches my eye and smiles. "But let me show you where you're staying. I bet you're tired, Rory, after that journey, and we're already losing the light."

Already? We set off so early. But Pia's right, the sun is barely above the horizon.

"Come, Laura, Rory, I'll walk you over to your building," Pia goes on. "You'll find it interesting, I bet. I see you have a camera? Pyramiden is a great place for photography."

My fingers clutch the yellow strap round my neck. "This was from my dad," I say, remembering the pride in Dad's voice as he handed me the reconditioned camera. "It was a present, so I can show him everything when we're home."

I turn to follow Pia when a grey flurry jumps round my legs, sniffing at my boots. It looks like a wolf cub, or a dog.

Mum steps back, alarmed.

"Ah, Kaiku!" an exasperated voice cries, and one of the children – a boy about my age – springs lightly on to the walkway next to me. "Come away!"

"Mikkal! Control your fox!" Pia cries, laughing.

A fox! Of course! Not a red fox like in the woods by Dad's, this one's smaller, with a pointed nose and thick glistening fur. But it was the colour that confused me. A shimmery grey, when I thought Arctic foxes would be white at this time of year.

"I don't mind, I love animals," I say quickly, bending down to stroke the little creature.

"Careful, Rory," Mum says nervously. "He might have rabies."

"*She*," the boy responds gutturally, glaring at Mum.

"Kaiku doesn't have rabies!" He gathers the fluffy creature up in his arms.

I attempt a smile but the boy turns his back to me deliberately, jumping down to the frozen ground. The grey fox is struggling in his arms, anxious to be free.

"Mikkal found Kaiku a couple of years ago," Pia explains. "He thinks her mother had been got by a bear. Mikkal hand-fed her and she's never shown any interest in going back to the wild."

"Mikkal," Pia calls, directing her words to the boy now. "I was going to ask a special favour of you – could you show Rory around? There are all kinds of things about Pyramiden you could show her that I still don't know about."

Mikkal stares back at me without saying anything. I shift my feet awkwardly, my toes squashed inside my new snow boots.

"Come on, Mikkal," Pia says persuasively. "Rory can tell you about life beneath the Arctic Circle. Aren't you always wanting to know about the big world out there?"

Mikkal gives a sullen headshake. "You know Jonne wouldn't forgive me, for spending time with one of the intruders." His words are spoken with feeling. Who is Jonne, I wonder? Is that how they see us, as intruders? I guess it makes sense they would.

"Ah, Mikkal," Pia says softly.

The boy keeps looking at me like I'm an alien that's landed in this strange place and he wants me to know exactly how unwelcome I am. Then the little fox manages to leap out of his arms and is back at my feet, jumping up again, higher this time, trying to scramble up my legs.

"Kaiku!" Mikkal shouts again, throwing up his hands in despair. "Do you learn nothing from our training?"

A tiny smile escapes from the corners of my mouth.

I bend down to stroke the grey fox, her breath hot on my fingers. She's exquisitely beautiful. It's a shame the boy so clearly dislikes me, because I'd love the chance to get to know her.

"Shouldn't she be getting her winter coat by now?" I can't resist asking. She should be white to camouflage against the snow.

"Kaiku's a blue morph. She stays the same all year," Mikkal answers, and then pulls a face, as though remembering he's broken some unspoken rule by speaking to me. He comes to retrieve his fox again. Blue, that's a better word. The way her fur shimmers like water. A blue fox in blue season.

I can't help laughing at Kaiku's deliberate jumps either side of the boy's open hands, determined not to lose her freedom.

Mikkal tuts loudly and, finally getting control of the fox, jumps from the walkway with a thud.

"Come away!" one of the older girls says. "Leave them."

She must be a couple of years older than me and has that presence I recognize from some of the girls at school. The leaders. The ones I avoid most.

She links arms with Mikkal, and the group walk en masse to a couple of swings in the middle of the square, piling on top of them like circus artists. They creak under their weight. Mikkal stands to the side, Kaiku still in his arms.

I watch, trying to squash down that feeling of being left out. An intruder.

"Don't worry about Mikkal, Rory," Pia says, patting me on the shoulder. "It's nothing personal. You seem to have won Kaiku over at least."

The older girl is whispering in Mikkal's ear and they look back towards me blankly. I hold their gaze, still feeling the warmth of Kaiku's breath on my fingertips. It's hardly fair that they're so unfriendly, especially when we just arrived here. But Pia's right, at least the fox is friendly. Maybe she can help me win the others over.

# Paris

Mark ushers Mum away and I'm left to follow Pia to Building Nine, the reality of accompanying Mum on a work trip starting to sink in.

After opening the door to the block, Pia flicks a switch on the wall. A few seconds later, a line of yellow strip lighting illuminates above us.

"Oh good!" she says brightly. "It's working now. The electricity in here can be erratic. This building runs off a separate generator, I think. It's – what do you say? – temperamental?"

"Who else stays here?" I ask. I have an odd sensation creeping over me, coming into the block. Homesickness. But something else too – something hanging in the air where we can see our breath like clouds.

"There are a couple of mine engineers on the ground

floor," Pia answers, taking her boots off and blowing on her fingers to warm them. "And now you and your mum, of course. I've put you on the third floor, so you get the view."

"Thank you," I say dutifully, taking my boots off too to leave on the metal grid by the door. My toes unsquash in my thick socks.

There's a rattling sound and Pia looks down the corridor absently. "It's the wind. You'll get used to it. They used to call this block Paris, and the one across the square, that was London." She points back out through the door, a wistfulness appearing on her face. "I sometimes wonder what it must have been like then. Maybe they had fancy parties and secret rendezvous!"

I look over to 'London' from the doorway. It could be a mirror image of this building – bare and rigid against the sky, which has turned a moody purple.

The children are still by the swings, but staring this way as if to watch how I react to my new home.

"Where do they all live?" I ask, tilting my head at them.

"The children?" Pia says. "Some live in the hotel, but most in that building over there."

I follow her finger to another of the uniform buildings.

"Some lived here too, in the beginning, but after more people left they mostly moved over there because the apartments have little kitchenettes. That block was built for families originally."

Pia slams the door shut and sets off walking along the tiled corridor in her socks. "Did you bring slippers, Rory? We always take our boots off because of the snow."

Through the glass I watch the children turn away and run off together.

I rush to catch up with Pia, keen to see our new home. We pass closed doors on either side and come to a staircase with a thin metal banister winding up to the higher floors. I glimpse empty rooms with peeling wallpaper, and odd chairs or bedframes, as we go up.

I've never seen empty space like this. Back home people would be crying out for these apartments, but then no one's meant to be living here at all, I remind myself. This is officially a wilderness.

"It's strange, isn't it?" Pia says, reading my mind. "When the mine closed both times, they say people left almost overnight. It's sad, really. Sometimes I imagine I hear their voices still."

We pause on the steps as the strip light flickers from the ceiling, as though someone's playing with a dimmer switch.

As we reach the third floor, Pia turns right before stopping halfway along the corridor. "Here we go," she says breezily, pushing open a heavy door.

The room inside is sparse – there's a metal-framed bed and an ancient-looking desk and chair, with a gold-jointed desk lamp on top. Mum will be pleased I have space to work! The curtains are yellow and the walls are covered in a pink paper of stretched diamonds. The floor's tiled with squares of brown and beige. Still, it's the most space I've had to myself since we left our old house.

"It's vintage, huh?" Pia says. "I'm not sure what the miners will think of these rooms. If Andrei's approval ever comes through." She gives a little laugh. "We need to get you more blankets for the bed, Rory. This room seems extra cold for some reason. There's a laundry room over in the hotel. You can collect some later, or someone will bring some over. I'm never sure whose job it is to do those kinds of things… They usually expect me to. The patriarchy never died in Greenlight." She rolls her eyes.

"I'll get them," I say quickly, hating the idea that I'd add to Pia's work here.

My attention is caught by a line of whale drawings, running along the wall at eye level. They're drawn in pencil on paper that's curled at the edges now. Below each whale, in tiny letters, is the species name.

I read the labels. *Beluga. Bowhead. Fin whale. Humpback. Minke. Narwhal.* They're all whales that are meant to visit these waters.

The narwhal's tusk spirals upwards like a unicorn's.

"I was going to take everything off the walls to give you a blank canvas, but I couldn't bring myself to remove these," Pia says.

I nod in agreement, transfixed by the swimming creatures. They are amazingly detailed and fluid. I wonder who drew them. Could it be one of the children we met? I decide the pictures look too old for that, and surely if the artist was still in town they'd have come back for them. Someone clearly spent a lot of time drawing them.

"I was hoping we might see whales from the *Leviathan*," I tell Pia. "We saw seals and walrus, but no whales."

"There's plenty of time for that," Pia says warmly. "More whales come into the fjords in autumn, I'm told. Maybe that will be a positive to your being here now and not the summer, after everything was delayed."

"I didn't know it was delayed," I say. Until a couple of weeks ago, Greenlight was just the name of an energy company back home.

"Ah, it was nothing," Pia says. "We thought it might all be off again and the other geologist left in a hurry. I don't think being here suited him."

She shivers and wraps her arms round her body. "Anyway, I guess that's when they found your mum to take his place. So it worked out well in the end."

"My mum's a replacement?"

Pia smiles briskly. "Yes, and we get you as a bonus! It's good to have fresh faces around here."

I move over to the window. Pia points landmarks out to help me get my bearings. To the left are more buildings –

the apartment block where she says the families live, and at right angles to that a 'Cultural Palace', whatever that is, with the stern statue in front and the dark triangular-faced mountain behind, with an old runway up to the mine. Then right, it's more buildings and the path stretching back to the fjord, and in the distance, across the water, the glacier.

The radiator's red-hot underneath the window – I pull my hand away with a gasp when I touch it – though for some reason the heat is hardly making it into the room. I can see my breath in little plumes of condensation.

The swings creak noisily back and forth in the square below. The children have disappeared.

"Those swings always blow in the wind," Pia says distractedly. "I'll get some oil on them later, or someone will. If you want to do something about this wallpaper, I've seen a stack of paint on the top floor of this building. There's loads of old junk up there but the paint looks like it might still be OK, if you fancy giving this room a makeover."

"Maybe," I muse. "But I'm only here a few weeks."

"I'm getting out before the true winter too," Pia says. "I don't know how the locals do it. Three months without seeing the sun at all." She shivers again.

"My dad says there will be starlight," I reply, "and moonlight, and the northern lights, if we're lucky."

"Oh yes, the *aurora borealis*! We've seen them a few times the last couple of weeks. It's like a green sea in the sky. It's very beautiful."

We smile at each other, though Pia's eyes are flicking to the door, as if she should already be somewhere else. "Will you be OK here? You could come across and explore the main building, the Cultural Palace. It was very grand here once, Rory! I'd spend more time showing you around now, but I have to go to that meeting your mum's been dragged to." She pulls a face like that is precisely not what she wants to be doing.

"Don't worry about me," I say, trying to sound light and breezy, like I'm perfectly accustomed to being abandoned by my mum a few minutes after arriving in an old Arctic mining town. "I can unpack and look around by myself, and … I'll be fine, I promise."

"If you're sure then. You must come and find someone if you need anything." She smiles at me kindly. "And don't let us forget about those extra blankets!"

"Honestly, I'll be fine," I assure her.

Pia looks relieved. "OK, Rory. I'll see you in the cafeteria for dinner. Everyone has all their meals there. Even the town children go there lately."

"Great," I say, despite the mention of the children making my gut twist a little.

"Oh, and Rory," Pia says, turning back in the doorway.

"You know the rules about the bears here? The main square is OK, but beyond that, even the outer buildings, you mustn't go without a rifle. You'd need someone to accompany you."

I nod back seriously. This place is most definitely a wilderness. Exploring it isn't going to be like walking in the forest by Dad's.

I unload my suitcase without much thought. It was such a last-minute whirl coming here that Mum mostly packed for me. I've not seen some of these clothes since last winter. I fold them up to put away in the chest of drawers next to the bed. The drawers stick in the frame and I have to use all my weight to get them to shut.

Out of my smaller backpack, I take my travel journal and place it on the desk, under the jointed old lamp. Later on, I'll sit down and stick in the Polaroid pictures I took on the boat.

The school textbooks Mum insisted we bring, I stack in the corner.

I catch sight of my reflection in the mirror as I get ready to leave.

My face looks solemn in the gilded frame and I practise smiling in case I run into any of the town children. They might not have drawn the whales on my wall, but I bet they know the best places to look for them.

# Palace

I see Mum coming towards me across the square and I breathe a sigh of relief. I didn't want to have to wander around strange buildings to find her.

"Rory!" Mum calls. "Did you hear there's a palace?!" She looks down at a wrinkled plan in her hands. "Shall we go and investigate?"

She takes my arm, and I lean into her gratefully. "Did you meet everyone?" I ask, genuinely curious about who else would choose to come and work out here.

Mum nods. "Yes! It's a larger team than I thought. There are quite a few mine engineers already. They've been doing some exploratory extraction. But the assessment team I'll be working with is small. Pia you've met. Isn't she lovely? Then Ingrid's the project administrator, she's pulling together all our reports and investigations for the approval. And Mark, of course. Apparently everything's to go through him so we don't stress out the big boss, Andrei." She rolls her eyes and I laugh.

As befits its name, the Cultural Palace is the largest building in the square, raised up and overlooking the fjord.

The door clangs shut behind us as we enter and we find ourselves in a double height hall with mirrored walls, and a central staircase leading to an upper floor, off which there look to be more rooms. On the ground floor, a couple of adults are sat on an old sofa. I can tell they're townspeople from the clothes they're wearing. Greenlight staff have new coats and thick trousers for the harsh weather. These two women are dressed in warm clothes too, but the fabrics are patched and worn.

Mum starts to walk over, smiling. The women bury their heads deliberately in conversation. When Mum tries to say hello, they barely acknowledge her. I watch her cheeks turn red in the mirrored walls and a lump rises in my throat.

"Shall we find the auditorium? Andrei wants to hold a public meeting there in a few days. I'd like to see it," Mum says and leads me through an open doorway.

As we go, charged voices and footsteps run through the main hall behind us. The children. Mum glances in their direction.

"How on earth did Greenlight miss them when they did their evaluation of this place?" she says thoughtfully.

"There are so many of them!"

I remember Nora in the airport, and the slightly sardonic way she talked about the Svalbard project. And Katerina in the restaurant, and that shopkeeper. None of them seemed to have a high opinion of Mum's new company.

"Maybe they left them out on purpose? To get their 'greenlight'?" I pun.

Mum's eyes meet mine, but she doesn't say anything.

We find the auditorium – a dimly lit theatre, with a podium at the front for a speaker – then walk through the sports hall, which has high basketball hoops. There's a room with books like a library and another with a piano. The piano has a couple of keys missing, and the remaining ones sound out of tune as I run my fingers over them.

Some rooms are empty, but others feel used and loved, with chairs and homemade blankets, and children's pictures on the walls, though none up to the standard of the whale drawings in my room. Every so often we hear more laughter or running feet.

We walk back across the square once we've finished exploring, the buildings around us flickering with yellow light. I think back to what Pia said about electricity being erratic here, especially in our block.

"They called it Paris once," I remember to tell Mum as we reach the door. It's only marked as Building Nine on her plan. The words feel a little ridiculous now. London.

Paris. They've lost the glamour they had when Pia said them. Those are places in some other world entirely.

I show Mum up to our third-floor rooms and we explore the length of the corridor together, and find a big, tiled bathroom with a free-standing bath.

Mum turns the hot tap to check it works. Steam comes off the running water and we both breathe audible sighs of relief.

"Can't complain at that, Rory!" Mum says, wringing her hands happily. "It must be saltwater. It'll be pumped up from the fjord before it's heated. It'll be like swimming in the Arctic Ocean every time you take a bath!"

She's less impressed by my room.

"I like it," I say defensively. It's strange but it already feels a bit like home, even though the temperature seems to drop a couple of degrees as we go in. "Pia said there's some paint upstairs, if I want to decorate."

"Good idea!" Mum says. "That would be a nice project while you're here."

I take the few short steps to the window. Flakes of snow are blowing sideways in the wind, drifting past the glass. I gaze out, remembering all the times in my childhood that I've longed for snow. Fat, soft crystals of it. I shiver.

"You're cold?" Mum says, placing her fingers on the metal radiator and looking around the room puzzled. "How can the heat not be radiating out to the rest of the room?"

I shrug. "Draughts, I guess?"

A solitary peal of laughter sounds just outside my door, and footsteps scurry along tiles. One of the children must have followed us in.

Mum doesn't appear to notice. She's studying the radiator, crouching down to see if she can get the dials on the side to turn. "The controls are painted shut. Still, I don't think it could get any hotter. The heat must go straight out of the window, maybe." She tuts. "We'll need to get more blankets, and a better mattress if we can. For me too. These ones are so thin." She presses her hand down on to the mattress and the springs inside creak painfully.

"Pia mentioned a laundry room, in the hotel," I offer.

"Well, that's good. Let's go over quickly before dinner."

"Shall I lock the door?" I ask, noticing a key hanging above the light switch.

Mum frowns. "I suppose so, with the resentment among the townspeople. That's why Andrei wants to organize that meeting, to try to get them on side. He's asked me to lead it."

"You just got here! Can't someone else do it?" I say, surprised at this information.

Mum smiles thinly. "I can't very well start laying down my terms already. He thinks they'll respond better to me because I'm new."

The thin orange strip lighting of the corridors barely seems to provide any illumination and for a few seconds it cuts out entirely. Mum and I run down the stairs. Our boots lie waiting for us on the metal grille by the door, where we left them. I wonder if this is the strangest place we'll ever call home.

# Stars

There are just a handful of Greenlight employees in the canteen. The townspeople must be eating in their apartments with their little kitchenettes.

I'm glad when Mum carries her tray to an empty table. It's good to have her to myself for a while. So much has happened today. I can't believe it was only this morning I was eating waffles with cloudberry jam! Pyramiden hardly seems like it could be the same island.

"I'm sorry for being quiet," Mum says, picking over her food. "My head's full of work."

"It's OK," I say, not minding the silence. I'm lost in thought too, still processing the journey over here, the harsh stares from the children and those unfriendly women in the Palace building. At least the fox seemed to like me.

The evening meal is a stew with potato dumplings.

Luckily there's a vegetarian version, though I reckon Mum's too distracted to even notice what we're eating.

Our feet skid on the icy path as we leave the canteen. Pia meets us coming in the opposite direction. "Laura! Rory! You've eaten already?"

"We need an early night," Mum says, smiling at her. "I want to get out to the new mine first thing tomorrow. Mark has arranged it, apparently."

"Oh yes!" Pia says. "I meant to be there to sit with you for dinner, I'm so sorry. I know this place can feel lonely in the beginning." Her words run into each other, each accompanied by a little burst of water vapour hanging in the night air.

"I understand, everyone's busy," Mum says.

"At least you two have each other." Pia smiles. "You're lucky. Have you looked at the stars yet, Rory?"

I tilt my head up. I've been so preoccupied with the people and the old buildings, I haven't thought to look up. I gasp. Even staying with Dad in the dark of the forest, I only saw a slither of this endlessness. It's like the whole of the galaxy is on display for us. A navy vaulted sky studded with beads of light.

"We didn't phone Dad," I say to Mum, hit with a pang of homesickness. I have so much I want to tell him already. We flew through the clouds! We're staying in Paris! There's a fox that's blue!

Mum's face falls. "Oh, the satellite phone. I haven't had a chance to ask about it yet." She looks at Pia for help.

"Can't you just call over the internet? From the office?" Pia asks.

"Not with Rory's father," Mum says, her teeth clenched. "He's off grid these days."

"Oh," Pia says surprised, but trying not to show it. "You could try the satellite phone, I suppose. I've never had reason to use it. I'm sure Mark or Ingrid or someone could help you."

"We'll try tomorrow, Rory," Mum says, squeezing my hand. "If only your father had internet like everyone else."

"It doesn't matter," I say, cutting Mum off. Dad's off-grid life is a source of contention between them. "Tomorrow will be fine."

I seek out Polaris. The North Star. It's located almost directly above the North Pole. Other stars seem to rotate around the Pole, but this one is always there, due north.

It's the brightest I've ever seen it.

It's what Dad used to call me, my pet name, when I was young. *My little North Star*, like I was both direction and guide, and something bright and shiny to be gazed at in awe.

"Well," Mum says, yawning now. "We should turn in. I have a busy day tomorrow."

"Sleep well," Pia says, and we part ways on the frosted walkway.

# Night

I was bone tired getting ready for bed, washing my hair in the warm salted water brought up from the fjord, but as soon as I lie down, sleep seems impossible. My mind twists and turns through everything I've seen today. Mum and I managed to get hold of more blankets, but we couldn't find any more mattresses and the springs of this one poke up into my back.

I turn to face the wall, where the whales swim in formation along the old patterned wallpaper. I can't paint it, I decide. Who knows how long the whales have swum through these pink diamonds?

I try counting stars like Dad taught me when I first started getting anxious about school. It worked best in his forest home because he made a skylight in my tiny room, cut out of the ceiling above my bunk. I didn't need to imagine the stars, they were all there above me. Dad convinced me I could do it in the town too, if I got my imagination to work hard enough. To fix the flecks of light in my mind's eye.

I get out of bed and go to the window now, peering out through the curtains, to see the stars again. They're as bright as ever, around the white crescent moon.

There's a sudden scurrying sound somewhere that I can't quite locate. I flick on the desk light and spin round sharply, because for a second I swear there's a face in the window. But that's impossible – we're three floors up.

It's a reflection I realize at once, surveying the empty room. There's just me, and the door to the corridor is firmly shut. Am I jumping at my own reflection now?

Just as I tell myself not to be silly, I hear a noise outside in the corridor this time. Maybe it's Mum on her way to the bathroom.

I make myself open the bedroom door. The corridor stretches away on either side, empty.

I come back inside the room to return to bed, but the mirror catches my eye. A face, I'm sure. A face that's not mine.

Terror flares inside me and I fly through the door and across the corridor to Mum's room. I rattle at the door handle. "Mum! Mum!" My voice echoes down the hallway.

More footsteps run down or up the steps, I can't tell

which. "Mum!" I scream.

Mum's looks pale when she opens the door, her brown hair tousling over her shoulders, her eyes creased with tiredness. "Rory, are you OK? Whatever happened?"

I fall into her arms. "There was a noise. In the walls," I cry. "And I saw a face, in the mirror."

Mum shakes her head sleepily, leading me to sit down on the bed next to her. "Rory, my darling. It's just dreams. Your mind must be unsettled after the journey."

"No," I insist breathlessly. "It wasn't a dream. I hadn't even got to sleep yet. I couldn't."

Mum glances at her wristwatch. "But it's past midnight. You must have been asleep."

"No!" I shake my head furiously. "I haven't. I've just been lying there. And then there was a noise, and the face, and someone was there, in the room with me. I swear it."

"No, my darling," Mum insists, her face full of concern. "The boat trip, new places, the cold." She goes on listing all the reasons my mind might be working overtime, and then takes me back to my room and makes a show of looking under the bed and opening the cupboard. There's nothing. No one.

"Rats, maybe, or mice?" Mum says, rubbing at her eyes, knowing animals don't faze me.

"I don't know," I say, my voice wavering.

"Go back to sleep, Rory. We'll investigate in the

morning," Mum declares with a loud yawn.

"I'm scared, Mum!"

She looks around hopelessly. "I'll stay for a while. I'll wait for you to get off to sleep."

She pulls back the covers and gestures for me to get in, before stroking my hair as I finally fall asleep for the first time in Pyramiden.

In the morning, Mum's gone, and when I get up to use the bathroom there's a book outside my room. I pick it up warily. So someone was up here. The book's proof of it.

*A History of Svalbard Whaling*, I read from the cover.

Perhaps Pia picked it up on her way out here, from the hotel in Longyearbyen. She might be worried I'll run out of things to do here.

I place the book on my bed, next to the whale sketches, thinking back to last night and how frightened I was. You get noises in old buildings. In new buildings too. Back home someone is always running a shower, or slamming a door, or playing music.

Still, I jump as Mum drums on my door in her familiar rat-a-tat-tat. "Rory! Breakfast!"

# Cafeteria

"How did you sleep?" Pia asks brightly, bumping into us as we go into the canteen.

"Rory," Mum starts, but I interrupt her.

"Fine," I answer. "We both slept fine." Last night seems an embarrassing overreaction.

"Why do the townspeople eat here if they're so against us?" Mum murmurs to Pia, as we join a small queue for hot food. This morning a couple of tables in the corner are occupied by settler families. I glance over with interest.

"Winter," Pia answers simply. "Winter is why they come. Some years their supplies run out. They've learned not to turn food away at this time of year. Like the reindeer, out there…"

"Reindeer!" I repeat loudly, my eyes jumping to the window. I go up to the glass.

There are two, outside on the grass of the square, using their noses to push away snow. Svalbard reindeer. I've been longing to see them. They're shorter and stockier than the reindeer you see on Christmas things, pulling Santa's sleigh. One turns to look at me, its eyes dark and intent, but a moment later goes back to tugging up whatever it's finding under the snow.

"From now until the end of October, the sun rises later and sets earlier every day, until the 26th, when it makes it above the horizon for a mere thirty minutes," Pia's telling us, bringing my attention back from the reindeer. "The day after, it doesn't make it above the horizon at all, and there is just the Polar Night until the sun starts to come back in late February."

"*Polarnatt*," I say, remembering the captain's word on the boat.

"Exactly," Pia says. "Or *mørketide* – winter darkness."

I shiver as we make it to the front of the queue.

The food at the hatch is decidedly fishy, despite the time of day. There is a stack of dry toasts beside it and slices of brown cheese. I think longingly of the hotel's waffles and cloudberry jam.

Mum hardly ever eats breakfast. She's reaching for a coffee pot, swirling steaming black liquid into her white cup.

I use the metal tongs to put a couple of the toasts on my plate and take my own mug of coffee.

"Are you sure that's enough food, Rory?" Pia asks. "You need to eat more when it's so cold outside. You don't want to try the fish? I know it must seem strange after growing up in the UK, but it's normal here. We eat it in Sweden too. It's better than bringing a lot of food over, and the fishing is very carefully controlled now."

"I just don't think I could…" I imagine the slippery, squishy texture of the fish in my throat. "Toast is good. I'm not that hungry," I finish, even though that last part is a lie.

We've only just sat down at the table but Mum's already looking at her watch. "I shouldn't stay long. I want to get over to the mine. I need to make sure I get enough hours of light."

The toast is dry and heavy in my throat. I look out of the window for the reindeer but they've moved away.

"You could sit in that building we explored yesterday, Rory? The Cultural Palace?" Mum goes on between sips of coffee. "You could take some school work over. Get off to a good start. Routines will be important here."

I look at Mum incredulously. It's our first full day and she expects me to sit down and do some school work!

"Can't I come with you?" I say at once.

Mum glances at Pia. "I don't think so. They're taking me in a snowmobile. I don't think there'd be space. You'll be OK here for a few hours, won't you?"

I nod, blinking quickly. This was the deal after all. We weren't coming for a holiday, not like we kidded ourselves on the plane. We're not on a clifftop in Portugal. We're in the Arctic wilderness and Mum's got a job to do.

The other children are sat at a table at the back, with big plates of food. They're laughing loudly.

"When is the pool open?" I ask Pia, getting a vision of clear water and the smell of chlorine. Swimming is one of my favourite things back home. It makes me feel weightless, and strong. Even after a bad day at school.

"The pool?" Pia says, surprised. "You were planning on using it?"

"Aren't we meant to?" I reply, blushing, because it's becoming clearer and clearer I've misunderstood this place.

"I don't think it's worked for years," Pia goes on. "Many things have fallen into disrepair. The town community haven't had the resources…"

"It doesn't matter, it was just an idea," I say, crunching on another bite of dry toast. The very idea of swimming here seems absurd now.

"I'm sorry, Rory. It was misleading of anyone at Greenlight to suggest…" Pia looks towards Mum for help.

"I'm realizing the UK office were quite sparse with the details they gave me," Mum says, trying to sound light.

"They didn't want to put you off," Pia says. She clanks her mug down on the table loudly. "I'm drinking too much of this stuff."

"I'll be happy looking around outside on my own," I say, remembering the reindeer.

Pia nods warily. "Only the very inner main square is safe without a rifle, though. You mustn't venture beyond it, remember, because of the—"

"Bears," I finish. I'm beginning to recognize a pattern. Am I going to see anything beyond old buildings and a square of frosty grass?

"Precisely!" Pia smiles apologetically. "I'm sorry, Rory. It's important you know how to be safe here. It's not like back home. Small mistakes can end badly."

"What about the other kids?" I ask. They don't look like they think of polar bears every hour of every day. They're laughing and nudging each other playfully. The boy with the fox is there and sees me looking over. I wonder where his fox is now.

"It's the same for them," Pia says, following my gaze. "They know to be careful. Not just for themselves, but for the bears too. No one wants a bear to be shot because someone's been careless."

"I would never put an animal in danger," I start, indignantly.

"Not intentionally of course," Pia continues, more lightly now. "We just have to think about our actions here. As it gets colder the children are spending more time inside anyway. Luckily they have lots of buildings to explore."

I nod. That must have been what I heard last night. A late-night expedition.

"I'm sure the children will be friendly once they get to know you, Rory," Pia adds, smiling at me kindly.

I suddenly remember the book on whaling. "Did you leave a book outside my door?"

Pia raises her eyebrows. "A book? I haven't been back to your building."

I shrug and look out through the window. The children have left and are walking out into the square. I watch them enviously, the easy way they have with each other. It must have been one of them who left the book. But why would they think I want to read about dead whales? It's living ones I want to see!

# Pool

I don't know who gave Mum the idea the swimming pool was usable. There's not a drop of water. The pool tiles are cracked and the silver ladders rusted. It looks like it hasn't been used in years.

I stand in the little spectator gallery picturing the pool filled with water, in the summer, light from a midnight sun streaming in through tall windows. There are three blocks with 1, 2 and 3 on – a little winners' podium. Did they have races here? I imagine the building filled with people after a day in the mines. Shouting, cheers.

I start to take photos on my phone, moving around the space to get the most interesting shots. Light bouncing off the green tiles. Ceiling beams of varnished wood. A wall of bold coloured squares and rectangles.

I startle as I hear something above me. A giggle, and a

little humming. There are two young girls, sitting a few rows behind me. They're maybe seven or eight years old.

"What are you doing?" one of them asks, with open-eyed curiosity.

"Just looking," I say. "Exploring."

I recognize them from the swings yesterday. They must be twins. They have the same straight black hair, swept back from their faces with simple hair ties, and the same bright eyes. I wonder how long they've been watching me.

"What are your names?" I ask, pleased they're speaking to me.

"Buppha," one girl answers, looking sideways at her sister, who stays silent and staring. "This is Nan. She's my sister."

"I can see that!" I smile.

They're tapping their feet against the floor and the whole seating structure rattles in the hollowness of the building.

"Did you ever swim here?" I ask them both, trying to make conversation.

Buppha shakes her head quickly as if frightened by the prospect. "We don't know how to. It's too cold." She gives a vigorous shiver.

I nod my head quickly. "Of course."

The quieter girl, Nan, is staring intently at my phone.

"Shall I show you?" I offer. "It's a phone but it's got a

camera on it, to take pictures. I could take your picture if you like?"

Nan shakes her head in alarm, and then Buppha pulls her up. "Sorry! We're not meant to talk to you."

They run off together and I'm left alone.

The pool building suddenly doesn't seem half so beautiful. I wander back into the Cultural Palace next door and through to the sports hall. There's a ball today, like someone might have just finished shooting some hoops. I take aim, but the ball bounces off the hoop and rolls to the side of the yellow floor.

I find the old school building, marked on the map Mum gave me, and wander over. There's a faded mural on the wall outside of a forest scene, which seems out of place here, in the starkness of the High Arctic.

Inside the classrooms are empty and I wonder why they're not set up for lessons, but that obviously isn't the way here.

Somewhere in the distance there's the sound of dogs barking, howling even, like wolves, though I know there are no wolves here. Maybe they're huskies. I determine to find out where they are. No one can tell animals not to talk to me.

I hear piano notes coming from the Cultural Palace and stroll back to listen. Some of the children are singing in a language I don't recognize. Norwegian? Russian? Finnish?

Mum told me there used to be a big Thai population in Longyearbyen, and Buppha and Nan sound like they could be Thai names.

The song's beautiful, but I hurry past the room it's coming from to a space underneath where the grand stairway sweeps up to the first floor. There's a frayed sofa, out of sight of the rooms above, and of the music room too, but still in listening distance.

I open my bag, taking out the book I found outside my room. As I turn the first page, a blue-grey flurry leaps on to my lap. "Kaiku!" I exclaim laughing, as she tries to lick my face.

"Ah, Kaiku!" a familiar voice cries. Mikkal stamps his foot when he sees me. Buppha and Nan are following and giggle loudly at the sight of Kaiku in the enemy's lap. The piano falls silent and more of the children flock into view. The little girl, Marnie, from yesterday, and the oldest girl too, her eyes wide and distrustful.

"Where did you get that book?" the older girl asks, standing over me.

I close it awkwardly, like I've been caught doing something I shouldn't. Kaiku turns to lick my fingers. "It was left outside my room this morning. Or last night. I heard footsteps." I scan their faces for blushes or knowing looks.

"We don't bother with Paris. We don't go in there," the

older girl says. The other children exchange meaningful glances behind her.

"So none of you left the book for me?" I press.

"Why would we leave you anything?" the girl says, her gaze intensifying. She sits on one of the seats opposite. "How did you sleep? You have shadows under your eyes."

I twirl my hair round my finger, wondering if I even remembered to brush it this morning. "There were strange noises. In the walls." I glance sideways again to check their reactions. "My mum thinks it could have been rats."

Mikkal laughs softly. "Svalbard rats, was it?"

I nod. "Or mice, maybe."

"Ah," he says. "The mice, yes!"

"The ice mice of Spitsbergen!" the older girl exclaims.

The kids explode into laughter, and the blush on my cheeks blooms bigger.

Mikkal looks at me uncomfortably. "Don't, Nina," he says. Then back to me. "We're just joking. It won't be mice or rats. There's nothing like that on the island."

I nod fast, kicking myself inside. I know that. Reindeer and Arctic fox are the only land mammals here, not counting the polar bear, which my book said was better counted as a sea creature. This isn't like being in the forest with Dad, where our hut is alive with all manner of creepy crawlies, and squirrels running over the roof, and wood mice finding their way in for food.

"There are noises sometimes," Mikkal goes on. "It's an old building. It does strange things at night. You should not worry."

"She should not worry!" the older girl, Nina, exclaims. "None of us would dare sleep in Paris. Everyone knows that's where the ghosts live. The island knows who's an outsider. It doesn't want them here. You're the one that said so."

Mikkal makes a slight shushing sound but keeps his eyes on me. "How long are you here for?"

"A few weeks maybe," I say. "Six, probably. Until the mine is approved."

The boy's eyes narrow. "The mine should never have come here. This isn't the place for it."

"They're doing it for good reasons," I say. "Greenlight, I mean. The world needs the earth metals, to move forwards again. For batteries, and smart phones and electric cars."

Mikkal holds my gaze and the blush comes back to my cheeks with a vengeance. *The world needs them?* I sound like Mum on the boat over here. "It's better than drilling for oil," I finish weakly, remembering what she said to the captain. "Or burning more coal."

"I hope you're ready for the dark season," Nina says ominously.

"What do you mean?" I ask, knowing there's something behind her words other than darkness. Some of the younger kids start to leave, bored of the conversation, or uncomfortable with it. The piano sounds again in the other room.

Nina shrugs. "You'll find out, staying in Paris. Don't say we didn't warn you."

The piano's louder now. The player must be really pounding those keys. Nina turns to leave, though Mikkal stays, probably because Kaiku is still here, settled snugly on my knee.

"What made you come here?" he asks, taking the seat Nina has just vacated. I think he expects Kaiku to make the leap across to his knee, but she stays put, refolding herself, stretching out her right foreleg so I can see the pads on her paws.

"My mum's a geologist," I start, but Mikkal pulls a face.

"Not your mum, *you*," he says. "You're not going to be working on the mine. Or is that your plan?"

"Of course not," I say, looking down at Kaiku as if to find my answer there. "I wanted a break," I say after a while, because he's evidently waiting for an answer. "I wasn't enjoying school. I don't fit in there." I'm surprised how liberating it feels to say this out loud. Here. When I'm so far away from it.

"What about your friends?" Mikkal asks bluntly.

I suddenly don't care what this boy thinks of me, at least not about *that* me, that girl at school. She seems so remote right now I can barely remember her. I look up at Mikkal.

"I had a friend once," I offer. "Betty. She moved away, a couple of years ago. After that..." My voice trails off, and I brush back my hair, my fingers catching in its tangles, remembering the scent of ice-cream rose petals.

Kaiku's fully asleep now, her pointed nose curled under her fluffy tail for warmth.

"What did Nina mean," I ask, "about the darkness, and Paris, and me finding out?"

"It's just what people say, about *polarnatt* here. They say the graves of Spitsbergen open as the winter comes."

"Who says?" I try and keep my face still.

Mikkal shrugs. "It's what people have always said about this place."

I keep on stroking Kaiku's soft fur. "But it's not true, is it? Darkness can't hurt you." And I don't believe in ghosts, I almost say, but for some reason the words stay on my tongue.

Mikkal shrugs again and gets up to go. The piano's fallen silent and the children are thronging out of the building. In another room someone is counting. They're playing hide-and-seek, I realize, like we used to in primary, even after we knew all the hiding places by heart.

"Kaiku!" Mikkal commands quietly and the fox gets up to follow him. They run out to join the game.

# Beluga

Mum catches me coming out of the canteen after a solitary lunch. "A guide's taking me up to see the old coal mine. Can you be ready in five minutes?"

"I can come?" I say, surprised even to see her. I thought that was Mum gone for the day.

"I had to come back from the new mine early. I got too cold. But I've put on extra clothes for the mountain."

"And I'm definitely allowed to come!?" My eyes travel to the mountain overshadowing the town, the site of the old mine.

"I didn't bother asking them," Mum says with a mischievous grin. "Now hurry!"

I rush back to my room to collect my phone, excited to be venturing outside of the town. This might be my chance to get close to one of the reindeer, or see more Arctic foxes.

Mum's waiting in the square. She smiles when she sees me coming. The noises last night seem unimportant now. It was first night nerves, or hot water cranking through old pipes, or cisterns flushing downstairs wherever those two mine engineers are staying. The stories about ghosts and graves are obviously just the children trying to scare me.

There's a man leaning against the stern-faced statue, whistling a tune that I recognize from the children's singing around the piano. Mum walks me over. "This is Ivan, Rory. He's lived here for years."

I gulp nervously. The man's one of the settlers then, the old miners, though he nods not unkindly at me, before heading off towards the mountain. Mum and I follow a few paces behind.

"Greenlight has employed Ivan as site historian," Mum explains. "He has first-hand knowledge of what used to happen here."

Ivan's striding ahead, not bothering to check our progress. Mum points to the covered passageway made of wood and corrugated metal that runs up the mountainside. "They call this the gallery. It's our way up."

"Is it safe?" I ask doubtfully.

Ivan laughs in a not entirely reassuring way. "It hasn't fallen apart yet."

I give Mum a sideways glance and she winks back at me.

"Did you bring torches?" the man says, pausing outside

the opening to the gallery. "The darker sections can be unnerving to some. Especially a child." His eyes meet mine, and I wonder what he'd say to Mikkal's little tale about the graves of Spitsbergen opening.

Mum flicks the switch on the head torch she's still wearing from her trip this morning.

"I've got my own," I say. I've already decided I'm not going anywhere on this island without my torch in my pocket. It's the one Dad gave me when he moved into his new place. It works on solar power, but has space for rechargeable batteries too and, in case either of those things fail, a wind-up handle. I flash it into the tunnel, lighting up rubble and discarded sections of pipe and cable.

We step over some of the rubble to enter and on to wooden flooring that slopes upwards, with raised tread marks at regular intervals. Parallel to the boardwalk is a set of rails, and for a split second, I imagine I hear trollies trundling down the incline, heavy with coal for burning.

Mum and I follow behind Ivan, our breathing getting heavier as we go up. Every so often we pause to peer out through gaps in the structure. We're gaining height quickly. No wonder we're out of breath already! The buildings of Pyramiden spread out below us, before the matt water of the fjord and the blue glacier beyond. I get the same feeling of awe as I did coming over here on the *Leviathan*. We're small and insignificant, eclipsed by the magnitude and starkness of the landscape around us. It's weirdly soothing.

"Is this thing moving?" Mum asks, grabbing hold of the handrail.

"Are you OK?" I ask, alarmed at how pale her face has gone.

"I'm fine! I just had ... a moment," Mum says, forcing a smile. "Dizziness. I need to catch my breath."

The walkway's swaying, blown in the Arctic wind, or picking up the reverberations of our footsteps, and I clutch the handrail nervously. It's worn smooth. From all the miners that will have touched it over the years, going up the mountain, to find their way down into its dark depths. But this structure has stood firm all these years, stuck tight to the mountainside.

I pick up one of the stray rocks from between the rails.

"They called it black gold," Ivan says, almost wistfully, staring at the chunk of coal in my glove.

"I can't believe they were able to mine it for so long," Mum murmurs, breathing more normally now. "The mine stayed open for several years after the Climate Laws, I think?"

Ivan nods. "People have always got away with things out here. The world doesn't see. Especially when money gets involved."

"Is that why the accident happened?" Mum presses.

"Lack of scrutiny?"

"The plane crash?" I ask.

Ivan shakes his head slowly. "That was before our time here. Your mum means the mine collapse."

My heart pounds a little faster. Collapse is not the word I want to hear halfway up a black mountainside, with ribbons of passageways beneath.

A gull screams overhead and comes down low over the tunnel. I watch it through a crack in the walls. We're invading its territory.

Ivan clears his throat to go on. "It was twelve years ago now. A section of the mine collapsed. It hadn't been supported properly. They were so keen to take out all the coal they could before someone stopped them. They cut corners. What did lives matter when there was so much money to be made?"

"Was anyone hurt?" I ask at once, knowing already what the answer will be. I see the pain in Ivan's eyes.

"There were many fatalities," Mum tells me, quietly.

I knew about the plane crash the first time the mine closed, but that seemed so long ago. I had no idea there'd been another disaster.

Ivan grunts. "More than a quarter of the town died. Almost all the workers we had, and a handful of children too."

"Children?" Mum gasps. "Surely there weren't children in the mines?"

There's a flash of anger from Ivan and the walkway trembles again as if it can still feel the repercussions. A landscape must remember something like that. "They were bringing lunches. They did it every day. The whole area blew up. It didn't matter whether you were deep down in the pit or up by the entrance. The mountain opened up and took you."

My blood runs a bit colder in my veins. Ivan clearly remembers every little bit of that day – his shoulders have become hunched, his eyes overly bright.

"That was why the mine shut finally that last time, many years after it should have done," Mum tells me softly. "It was a terrible tragedy."

"Will it be safer this time? The mining?" I ask Mum, overcome with new fear.

"This is different altogether," she answers quickly. "The rare earths are much more accessible than coal. The new mine is only a few metres down."

"Your mines come with different problems," Ivan voices.

Mum purses her lips. "Greenlight picked the site carefully, to minimize damage to the tundra. Our extraction methods are cleaner than ever."

Ivan raises his hand dismissively. "This is an argument for another day. The town are waiting for your presentation. It's tomorrow night, yes?" His eyes fix on Mum intently. She hadn't told me the meeting would be so soon.

"We came to look at the rocks," Mum says, smiling at me now. "Let's at least get to the top."

We emerge from the structure two thirds of the way up the mountain and stand amid leftover bits of metal and machinery. You can see sunken bits of terrain, which must be where the mine collapsed.

Ivan slumps down at the entrance to the gallery, rifle over his shoulder, and takes a dog-eared book from his pocket.

The sun's sinking towards the horizon. Is the light always dying here? The sky's a dusty pink glow, the mountaintops blue, the glacier in the distance bluer still.

I wander around the mountain slope snapping photos with my phone. We could be on Mars here. We could be as far away as that, it's so different from my life before, where the school day will still be in progress.

Mum's gone into one of her thoughtful silences and is scooping up different coloured rocks – copper browns, midnight blacks, every shade of grey. It reminds me of the holidays we took when I was small, to Whitby and Robin Hood's Bay. The beaches where Mum taught me to look for fossils in the grey shale. Not just the spiral ammonites, but shells called devil's toenails; tiny, starred crinoids; even bones of giant sea reptiles.

I wind my scarf tighter round my neck. The wind's sharper up here and carries tiny shards of ice.

One of the mine shafts you could walk right into.

There are discarded wooden planks where it was blocked off once, but they've been broken away, or have come loose in the wind. It looks level for ages inside, until it becomes too dark to see. The ground is hard and smells like metal.

"I wouldn't go in there," Ivan says, raising his voice from where he's still sat, book in hands.

Mum calls over, concerned. "No, Rory, you mustn't go in! We don't know how stable it is. We didn't even bring hard hats."

I walk in the opposite direction, where several wooden crosses are silhouetted against the sky.

I look towards Ivan, to see if he's going to warn me away from here too, if they're memorials, or graves following the mine collapse, but his attention is back on his book.

My eyes pick out something by my feet. A strange smooth whiteness in all the grey scree and leftover bits of coal. I scoop it up in my glove.

It's a tiny whale figurine. It's carved out of bone, I reckon. The whale's a beluga, I'm guessing from the roundness of its shape, and the sort of smile – friendly and curious. The white whales of Spitsbergen, the belugas are called in my book.

What on earth is a beluga figurine doing up here by the coal mine?

I look around to show Mum, or ask Ivan about it, but

they're both head down in their different worlds. Mum in the rocks and seams of the mountain, the man in his book.

I push the whale into the pocket of my trousers. Maybe I'll question Pia about it when we next see her. Or even Mikkal, if I'm brave enough. Someone must know something about such a pretty carving.

# Allegiances

"You'll sleep better tonight," Mum tells me, her arm in mine as we make our way back from the canteen after dinner. "After that walk up to the mine, I bet you'll drift off right away."

"I wish I could have spoken to Dad," I say.

"They'll look into it. Ingrid promised, didn't she?" Mum assures me.

"Did she?" I ask, because that's not really what I got from the awkward encounter in the Greenlight offices. Ingrid did her best, I suppose, but there was general bemusement at Mum's request to use the satellite phone. It never works, was the gist. What if I don't get to speak with Dad the whole time we're here? Would he think to go to the town library and send an email?

"Pia didn't have dinner with us again," I brood.

"Even though she said she would." Pia was in the canteen all the time we were, but stayed at a table in the corner with Ivan and a couple of younger townspeople.

Mum smiles fondly. "Pia can't be at our beck and call. She's young. She's got her own life here. It's good she's got to know some of the residents. It was Pia who persuaded Ivan to take the position of site historian. The Arctic Council made that a condition of Greenlight's licence, once they realized the extent of the mining community left in Pyramiden."

I shrug, knowing I sound petulant. It's because it feels too familiar from school – sitting alone at a table, picking at lunch, while everyone else is surrounded by friends, conversation and laughter. I don't know how it even became like that. When I started at secondary school, I was so buried in everything happening at home, the swamp of Mum and Dad's separation, I didn't make much effort. I wasn't fussed who I was with or where I sat, and then when I was, it was too late. Allegiances had formed. Tight groups and just a few outliers like me, who don't fit anywhere. I wish for the millionth time that Betty's family hadn't dragged her away for a new life on the coast. But maybe it would be different between me and her too now. Maybe something just happens when you get older that I haven't kept up with. New ways of acting and being.

Mum and I have stepped off the walkway to stand in the

centre of the square and are gazing upwards, revelling at the brightness of the stars in the pitch-black sky. I can feel the frozen ground through my snow boots and the cold boring through my coat as well, but neither of us seems to want to go back yet.

"I've got that meeting tomorrow, for the townspeople," Mum voices.

"Are you nervous?" I ask. It's too dark to see Mum's expression, but her silence works its way through me.

"I still don't understand why they're making you talk anyway," I protest. "Can't someone else do it?"

"I told you, Andrei and Mark think a new face will be good. The townspeople have taken against the rest of them."

"Not Pia," I say at once, thinking of her back in the canteen, laughing with Ivan and the others.

"No." Mum laughs softly. "Not Pia. But I don't think Andrei would trust her to speak. Ingrid told me he thinks Pia's lost her loyalty to Greenlight."

"Why does Pia need to be loyal anyway?" I ask. "Aren't you all just telling the truth?"

Mum squeezes me towards her and I melt into her, grateful for the shared warmth as we step back on to the walkway to head over to Building Nine. "Oh, Rory, I am grateful to have you here."

"Are they not being nice to you?" I say suspiciously.

Mum laughs. "It's not like that. Everyone's just stressed and tired. Andrei's got a bit paranoid. He so wants this to be a success. Green energy is his life's work. He knows it won't continue without projects like this, to provide the rare earths."

"Then he should address the townspeople tomorrow," I say, my teeth clenched with a mixture of cold and injustice. I hate seeing Mum under pressure.

We use the bathroom together, cleaning our teeth at the sink, washing our faces, even though the water is cold tonight.

"The boiler must have cut out. I'll talk to someone tomorrow," Mum says with a yawn. "I can't face it tonight. The radiators seem to be working at least. We both need a good night's sleep, Rory!"

I glance at her quickly, wondering if there's an implication in her words, that she doesn't want to be disturbed the night before a presentation. Whatever noises or strange visions tonight brings, I vow to stay in my room with the whales.

In bed, I turn the pages of the whaling history book. I read about a Dutchman discovering the archipelago in 1596, and seas so full of whales, walrus and seals that ships had to break their way through. Did the crew of the ships marvel at the creatures? They must have done. But they saw them as a way of making money too – enough oil to power all the lights of Europe, the book claims.

After a few pages, I turn away from the gruesome illustrations of whales with harpoons sticking out of them and fjords running dark with blood. I stare at the sketches on the wall next to me instead, surprised at how much comfort they bring me. They're so lifelike. The bowhead is just like the figurine I found up at the mine, with its happy cartoon-like smile.

# Assembly

Mark has arranged a huddle of chairs in the auditorium for the meeting. It doesn't take long before they all fill up and families start dragging more chairs across from other rooms, or sit on the floor. The children are here too. Even the little ones who have no idea what it's actually about. Bhuppa and Nan sit cross-legged on the floor, next to a couple of boys and tiny Marnie. This is entertainment for them.

I sneak in to sit on the floor underneath one of the windows. An icy draught blows down my neck and I'm glad I kept my coat on. I look around for Pia but there's no sign of her anywhere.

Mum stands at the podium, before a broken mosaic on the wall. I'm not sure how I didn't notice it the other day. It's a panorama of icy sea and mountains, with polar bears

– a mother and her cub – and a Norse god with flowing white hair, all under a blazing midnight sun.

The settlers are grunting to themselves. It's not going to be an easy audience to win over.

"If I can take a moment to explain the plan for the proposed site," Mum's saying politely, rapping her knuckles on the podium and clearing her throat loudly when the background noise doesn't cease. She ratchets up the volume. "It is in everyone's interests to understand the geology at play here, the relative positions of the town and the fjords and the metals."

There's jeering from some of the audience and laughter from the children.

Mum's shoulders clench together and she tries clapping her hands, like our teachers used to back in primary. Out of the corner of my eye I spot Mikkal. He's snuck Kaiku in and she's asleep on his knee. He's sat next to a woman with grey hair and eyes just like his. His mum, I suppose.

A loud gong clamours through the room behind me.

Everyone looks back. A young man has climbed up to the wall where a bronze disc of metal is hanging. He hits it again with a padded mallet that hangs next to it and a hollow tone resonates around the room.

Someone crouches down beside me. Pia. "I'm hiding," she whispers, winking. "So they don't get me to speak!"

As the man with the gong starts talking, I realize where I recognize him from. I've seen him with Pia in the canteen. He's from the town but the two of them are obviously friends. No wonder Pia's hiding, if she feels split between the different factions.

The man's voice is not particularly loud, yet you could hear a pin drop in the room. "We should give her the courtesy of listening," he says calmly, indicating my mum. "We may not agree with the situation the Arctic Council has imposed on us, bringing in this company, but we should give her this courtesy. Laura. She is an expert in rocks and minerals."

Mum nods at him, surprised and grateful. "Thank you," she breathes. "Mr…"

"Jonne," the young man answers. "My name is Jonne."

Mum catches my eye and I nod encouragement at her.

Jonne takes a seat at the back. Pia stays still beside me.

Mum shuffles her papers nervously. "I've been brought in to help with the final assessment of the mine site. We're hoping the Arctic Council will visit soon to make their approval, after which mining can begin in earnest."

There's a roar of disruption. People shouting that the mining's already begun. That Greenlight are lying.

Is that true? I remember the containers waiting on the dockside when we arrived, being loaded on to the *Leviathan*, bound for Longyearbyen, then back to who knows where. Halfway across the world probably, just like the coal was for all those years and years, even when people knew the damage it was doing.

Mum's looking to the side of the room for support from colleagues, to counter the hostility in the room. None of them come forward. I bristle with anger at their still faces: Andrei, Mark, even Ingrid, who Mum insists is being nice to her.

There's a steady drumming of feet on the wooden floor. Calls about the mining being unsafe, something about it bringing death to the island.

Mum puts her hand up to quieten the room again. "Any work so far has been exploratory, and in the terms of our initial licence. We need to see the full lifecycle of the process. We are confident that here, in the icy wilderness of Spitsbergen, it is the ideal place for this kind of operation. This island can actively contribute to green technology. It can be at the forefront of the green economy."

Mum's trying to sound upbeat, to bring them round. "There could be real benefits for your community here. Jobs, for the first time in over a decade. We could look to reopen a school, for your young people." She gestures to the row of little kids at the front. "Greenlight has not come to exploit this place. We are operating as part of the Wilderness Preservation Act. We are fully aware of what's at stake here."

She's louder now, taller, and I can't help but feel proud of her, addressing a room of people with completely contradictory views. The drumming of feet has lessened and I notice Mikkal's mum straighten at the mention of a school.

Then, for no apparent reason, Andrei gets up and waves Mum to the side, sighing with annoyance. Pia stiffens beside me. "That man!" she hisses under her breath. "Your mum was doing really well."

"The world is hungry for rare earths," Andrei shouts above the renewed clamour. Clearly they all dislike him. "For green energy, for batteries and electric cars, for electronics, for smart phones. If you took your place back in the real world, you would be hungry for them too."

The jeers get louder. What are those things to people here?

The gong sounds again. Pia's friend, Jonne, is up on his chair now, his eyes bright. For a second, they travel across the room to where I'm sitting, Pia beside me. I swallow. Then he turns his eyes on his own people. "This place has been plundered before. First they came for the whales and the walrus. Then it was furs, from polar bears and foxes. We know the history of this place too well."

As if she's listening, there's a tiny yelp from Kaiku, awake now, and skittering round Mikkal's feet lightly.

Jonne's voice goes on. "Then it was coal, dug from the

bowels of the mountain. We all know what happened there: first the plane crash, for the people before us, and then the collapse, in our time. Our lifetimes, where we lost family members and friends. Why should we believe this company, Greenlight, and these newcomers who have not even taken the time to get to know our island? Why should we allow it to be plundered again?"

Mum meets Jonne's gaze head on but doesn't say anything.

"Look at the mosaic behind you," he says, as if addressing Mum personally now. "The polar bears are recovering, and even the whales, out there." He gestures his hand out towards the fjord. "The world set this place aside as a wilderness. Was that just a game, a joke? How few years before you come back to destroy it all over again?"

Mum shakes her head. "The Arctic Council would not have given Greenlight permission to mine here had they not been certain that the very best international practices are being followed. This is precisely why we're undertaking such a comprehensive environmental impact assessment."

"How can they know what's happening out here?" someone shouts from the audience. "Out here no one sees. Especially the way your company works." It's Ivan, from yesterday's visit to the mine. He's sat next to Nina. Seeing them together, the family resemblance hits me. He must be her dad.

Nina's eyes meet mine and I raise my eyebrows. Why has she got it in for me when in a roundabout way she has a parent working for Greenlight too?

"I don't see you turning down your payment cheque at the end of the week, Ivan, our *site historian.*" Andrei sneers as he addresses him. "Greenlight will provide many more jobs, *real* jobs, for your sons and your daughters when our mine is running."

"If you get your licence through," Ivan retorts, unperturbed. "You keep telling us the delegation from the Council is coming. Well, where are they? Have there been more delays, as you find new people who will stick to your story script?" At this, Ivan's eyes irrefutably travel to Mum, and I sink down, away from Nina's reproving gaze.

Jonne's speaking again, his voice clear from the back of the room, and I feel Pia tense beside me. "You picked a wilderness so there is no one to see. But you chose wrong with Pyramiden. We are here! We are watching! We see your new roads, destroying the tundra. The scars you leave on the earth. We see the Svalbard reindeer fall sick and die at the bottom of the mountains."

Blood rushes to Andrei's cheeks. "Not those claims again. We have expert evidence that that is a population imbalance in the reindeer and in no way related to our mine."

"They are not dying of hunger. Something is poisoning them!" Jonne insists.

Mum looks confused and uncomfortable beside her boss. It seems like it's the first she's heard about any of this.

"That is impossible," Andrei storms. "Our methods of extraction are the purest and most efficient on the planet. We will leave no trace."

Jonne's having none of it. "You believe you can hack elements from under the ice without consequences for the wildlife here? For the people who have made this place their home? You think people can carry on taking riches from the earth and there is not a price to pay?"

I glance sideways at Pia, but she has eyes only for Jonne. As Andrei becomes louder and more aggressive, Jonne maintains his calm, steely composure, and soon Greenlight's control is lost. The meeting descends into chaos. Andrei starts gesturing that it's over.

I stand up, knowing I should go to the front, to Mum, but I can't bring myself to. I leave her gathering up her notes and run outside.

# Reindeer

I walk across the square, keen to get some fresh air and disappear out of view for a while, when a hand taps my shoulder, the same instant I trip over a soft moving mass. Kaiku!

"Hi," Mikkal says.

"Hi," I reply warily.

"Will your mum be OK?" he asks. "She looked upset."

I hug my arms round my body, touched that he's asking about her. "They shouldn't have made her spokesperson," I say. "Not so soon."

Mikkal opens his mouth to say something, then shuts it again.

"Is it true, about the reindeer?" I ask, crouching down to Kaiku, her wet trusting little nose. Straight away she's up on my lap, pressing into me. I cuddle her closer.

Mikkal glances either side, as if to check no one's noticing him talk to me. "I can show you if you like?"

I get to my feet, taking my own furtive glances back to the Cultural Palace. Maybe there's a way I can help Mum find out what's really going on here. I don't trust Andrei or Mark or any of the others.

Mikkal gestures for me to follow as he slips between two of the grey brick buildings.

"Is it safe?" I ask. I don't have to spell out what I mean. Mikkal nods at once, though I notice his eyes scanning the tundra behind the buildings.

"The bears wouldn't pick this side to come into town, where the dogs are."

"I've been hearing the dogs, at night," I say, not mentioning the other noises I've been hearing. I didn't disturb Mum last night, but I heard the same footsteps again, and a voice somewhere out in the corridor. A girl's voice, I'm certain of it. I pulled my blankets up to my nose and pretended it wasn't happening.

Mikkal smiles with obvious affection. "They're loud this time of year. They're waiting for a proper snowfall so they get a good run on the sleds."

"Are they huskies?"

"Huskies, Lapphunds, crossbreeds. They're all sorts." He grins at me. "They look like wolves, most of them!"

"But they're friendly?"

"Providing they're not hungry!" He winks to show he's only half joking at least.

The barking intensifies as we approach a set of huts behind one of the buildings. There's a kind of greenhouse too, with green plants pressed against the glass.

"Rasmos found some sick reindeer," Mikkal tells me. "He's looking after them."

We're at a yard of thronging brown, grey, white, black and tan creatures, all with tongues hanging out, wagging tails and shining eyes. Mikkal puts his hand over the gate and is licked by a dozen different tongues. They're straining to reach me.

"Are you scared?" Mikkal asks, puzzling over my hesitancy. "They know you're new here. They want to get a sniff of you."

"No, not scared exactly," I say, despite my heart hammering in my chest. The dogs seem so loud and wild. I edge closer and put my hand over the gate to touch their rippling fur. They tremble excitedly. "They're beautiful," I murmur, my stomach giving a flutter of delight.

A man pokes his head out of one of the hut doors to eye me suspiciously. I wonder if he was at the meeting just now.

"I brought Rory to see the reindeer," Mikkal explains, before the man can say anything. "How are they doing, Rasmos?"

The man tilts his head to the largest hut. "We'll lose

them, I think. I should stop feeding them now."

Mikkal's face falls and he steps towards him. "No! Not yet, Rasmos, surely? I can help you look after them."

Rasmos lays his hand on Mikkal's shoulder, his voice gentler now, seeing the boy's distress. "Leave Kaiku in the yard, so she doesn't frighten them, yes?" Mikkal chucks Kaiku over the gate to the dogs and I brace myself for her to be swallowed up whole, but the dogs surround her in a happy circle of wagging tails.

Inside the hut, two reindeer are lying side by side. They're clearly very sick. Even the air in the hut smells of sickness. I put my hand up to my mouth, struck by an awful desire to leave. These reindeer are nothing like the ones I've seen already, wild and solid on the frozen earth between the buildings of Pyramiden.

Mikkal drops down beside the two creatures, deflating. "They've got worse," he murmurs. "Yesterday they were eating a little and I hoped..." He swallows.

"What's happened to them?" I whisper, afraid I'll scare the weakening creatures.

"This is what Jonne meant, in the meeting. More and more reindeer are getting sick. No one knows why. Or no one will tell us why."

"Why do you think it's to do with Greenlight?" I ask.

Mikkal's eyes narrow. They're the same colour as the fjord outside. "You're the miner's daughter. You must know about rare earth mining."

"My mum's not a miner," I say quietly. "She's a geologist. She studies rocks and landscapes and…" I have this urge to tell him about Mum's desk back home in our apartment. Her partitioned shelves of rocks and crystals.

"Greenlight employed her," Mikkal interrupts. "She must know what they do. Surely you know too? The chemicals that they use to take out the metals poison the tundra and wash away into the sea. Jonne says in a decade Greenlight will be done with this place but their chemicals will be left for a thousand years."

"No," I say, shaking my head again. "That's not how it is. Greenlight aren't using chemicals here, they're using some kind of bacteria." My brow crinkles and I wish I'd listened more attentively to Mum's explanations about the new technology they're employing here. "The Arctic Council wouldn't allow them to work here if it was damaging."

Mikkal's face becomes angry. "Where are the Arctic Council now? Why aren't they here, looking at these reindeer, watching them die?"

I put my hand out tentatively, to stroke the reindeer closest to me. Its eyes are closed, and ribs protrude out of its chest. Its skeleton pushing its way out before the poor creature's ready. I shudder. I'm sure the reindeer feels colder than it should.

"I read in my book that sometimes their teeth wear

down, when they get older, so they can't chew the plants to eat," I start to say.

"They're not starving, Rory," Mikkal says through gritted teeth. "These two aren't even that old. It's the mining, we know it is." He smooths down the fur of the reindeer next to him. Its flank trembles. "It's something they're doing. It's not at the main mine site, it must be somewhere else. We've been trying to find out where but we can't work it out. It could be anywhere. Greenlight are so secretive."

I keep my eyes on the reindeer, not knowing quite what to say. Mikkal talks gently to the creatures, slipping into Norwegian. Their breathing slows a little, responding to his voice and his touch.

I blink back salty tears. Could a green energy company really be poisoning a wilderness? Surely Mum wouldn't work on a project where that was even a remote possibility?

"Are these ones male?" I ask Mikkal. The reindeer's antlers are branched like trees and velvety like moss.

"Females," he says. "Both of them. The boys have bigger antlers, though they'll be losing them soon. These girls would keep theirs all winter, to protect any babies they have in spring. If they make it, that is."

He picks up a piece of heather from the floor and offers it to the reindeer, but they both turn away.

"Have you shown them to the Greenlight people?" I ask.

"We've tried. Ivan, Rasmos, my brother."

"Your brother?" I ask, the faces of the other children running through my head. "I didn't know you had—"

"Jonne," Mikkal interrupts again.

"Oh," I say quietly. "Him. The man with the gong. I had no idea." Though I see it now – Mikkal's a younger version of his brother. They have the same dark eyes and thick eyebrows, underneath tousled blond hair.

"Only Pia listens," Mikkal goes on. "A couple of the others came to look at the reindeer but they refuse to believe this is something new, or else they lie." His voice drips with resentment.

"What about Pia? Can't she do something?"

Mikkal shrugs. "Greenlight don't trust her since she became friends with Jonne. There are things they're not telling her."

I've left my phone in my room charging, but I pull out the Polaroid camera from round my neck and snap a photo of the reindeer. "I want to show my mum. I'll get her to come here too, to see for herself."

Mikkal watches as the little yellow machine whirrs and feeds out a square of film.

"It's a Polaroid," I explain. "It doesn't save the pictures, it prints them for you, see?"

I hand the photo over to him to take a proper look. Mikkal turns it over quizzically, as if he can't quite believe the image appearing before him. It seems a weird kind of magic out here.

The dogs are howling louder now outside and I glance towards the doorway.

"Can we go and see them again?" I'm suddenly desperate to be out of this building that smells so much of sickness and death.

"You go. I'm staying with the reindeer. It's best anyway that we don't hang out together," Mikkal says.

I jolt in surprise at these last words, and a familiar sickness worms its way into my stomach.

"It's just how it is here," Mikkal explains, watching my face fall. "My brother wouldn't like it. Or Nina. She lost her mum in the mine collapse. She hates mining companies."

"I get that. But Greenlight is a totally different company, and Nina's dad works for them now. I met him. He took me and Mum up to the old coal mine."

Mikkal shrugs. "Ivan thought if we cooperated, Greenlight would allow us to stay. But that was before the reindeer got sick and it became clear we couldn't trust them."

I remember Ivan on the mountainside, deep in his book. It must be so painful to revisit the site of the disaster. And for Nina, to live in the shadow of the mountain where her mum died.

"Did you lose family too?" I ask Mikkal tentatively.

Mikkal's posture changes and his eyes flick away from me.

"Two brothers. They both worked down there." He pauses, his eyes back on the reindeer. "And my dad. If Jonne was a year or two older, he'd have been down there too. I was just a baby."

"I saw the crosses up there," I say inadequately, not knowing how to convey how sorry I am for everything this boy's family has been through.

Mikkal shrugs. "The mining company pulled out of this place straight away and left. But it was too soon for some people, to leave their dead families like that. They put the crosses up to remember them. Everyone said the mining company was glad we stayed," Mikkal says bitterly. "They didn't want us going back and telling the world about the disaster they caused. They were happy for us to be forgotten about instead."

I remember the whale figurine I found up at the mine and dig it out of my pocket to show him. "Do you know what this is? It was up by the crosses."

Mikkal gazes at the beluga with clear recognition. "Jonne," he says, his voice pained. "My brother." He looks away.

"It's his?"

"He carves them out of whale bone. For his friend."

I stare at Mikkal quizzically, not understanding.

"Ulya, she was called. She died too that day in the accident. She was fourteen, not much older than us.

Jonne's never really..." Mikkal hesitates as if finding the right words. "Let her go," he finishes.

"Ulya," I say, repeating the girl's name sadly. It rings around the musty shed.

"Jonne leaves the whales like an offering. Mum says he and Ulya used to watch for them, from up by the mine. It was the best vantage point for seeing the fjord. Jonne still goes up there to talk to her." Mikkal's eyes remain guarded, as though daring me to laugh or taunt.

I don't know why he thinks I would. Tiny hairs stand up on the back of my neck, thinking about Jonne and Ulya as children, climbing up to the mine to go whale watching, not knowing what tragedy was going to rip their lives apart. And Jonne here now, all these years later, grown up, still making gifts for his childhood friend. Sadness wraps around me.

"I shouldn't have taken it. The beluga, I mean," I say reproaching myself. It feels greedy now, to have taken the whale for myself.

"Ulya's dead, isn't she?" Mikkal says curtly. "She won't miss it. Mum says Jonne should concentrate on the living now." He wrings his hands miserably.

I nod in agreement, though I vow to return the whale as soon as I get the chance. It's cold in my fingers, like it's made from ice, not bone.

# Northern Lights

I track through the ground floor of the hotel building to the Greenlight offices. Ingrid is in the main office room where the fans of the ancient computers whirr noisily.

"Do you know where my mum is?" I ask, poking my head in.

Ingrid smiles. "Hiding from Andrci, probably! He was cross with her after the meeting."

"But that's not fair!" I snort. "Mum did her best. If he hadn't interrupted her it might have gone better!"

Ingrid shuffles some paperwork on her desk. "Well, that's Andrei for you. Nothing's ever quite good enough, and nothing's ever his fault."

My eyes wander to the satellite phone out in the corridor where it was left yesterday. My hopes of speaking to Dad today fade.

"I'll get one of the engineers to take another lo[ok]" Ingrid says, kindly now, indicating the broken pa[rt]. "I'm sure there's a way. It shouldn't be rocket science."

I smile gratefully. "I'll go find my mum."

"Good plan, lovely. Let me know if she needs anything[.]"

Outside, snow's falling in icy splinters that sting m[y] face as I cross back to our building. I glance across at th[e] canteen. The windows are steamed up and there's the usual clatter of serving plates and chatter. It seems extra loud tonight.

I find Mum in her room, lying down on her bed.

"Rory!" she says, sitting up and wiping her brow. "I had a headache. Where did you end up? I looked for you."

"One of the children took me to see some reindeer." I sit down on her bed next to her, keen to tell her everything.

"The reindeer?" Mum asks, pulling her knees up to her chest.

"Sick ones, like they were talking about in the meeting. They've got two up by the dog sheds. They're dying, Mum." I hand her the square photo I took in the hut.

"I don't know what I'm supposed to be looking at," Mum says, peering at the murky picture.

"The reindeer, Mum!" I say, exasperated now. "I s[aw] them!"

Mum nods at me gently. "I see, Rory. It must be s[ad to] see them like that, but I've had assurances that an[y]

reindeer have nothing to do with the mine. Every year some will die as the weather gets colder. It's a natural fluctuation. In the winter there's not food for all of them."

"No," I say helplessly. "No, I asked about that, and anyway if you saw them, you'd realize. Plus Mikkal and Jonne and Rasmos and the others, they know the reindeer better than anyone. They wouldn't get this wrong."

"Jonne?" Mum says, her expression darkening. "Is that the same Jonne who took control of the meeting I was meant to be leading?" She rests her hand back on her forehead. "I understand their position. They resent us coming here, threatening this place they've managed to keep to themselves all these years. Andrei's annoyed I wasn't more assertive with them at the meeting."

I frown. "But I thought the meeting was for the townspeople, so they could put across their concerns. You had to let them speak, didn't you? That was the whole point of it."

Mum smiles thinly. "None of it's for you to worry about, Rory. I just need to write my geological report for the Arctic Council's assessment. The sooner it's done the better, for everyone."

"I could help you," I say keenly now, sitting up straighter. "If you want to find out more about the reindeer. I could show you them, you could speak to Rasmos. He seems nice."

"No, Rory," Mum says, shaking her head. "Do you not understand what I'm saying? It's important you stay out of it. The last thing I need is you disrupting things. They're behind where they wanted to be and if the Arctic Council don't approve the mine on this next visit, Andrei says they'll withdraw the licence altogether. Or the investors will pull out."

I screw my face up. How can Greenlight simply dismiss the views of the people who know this place best? I could growl in frustration.

I decide that if Mum doesn't have time to investigate what's happening to the reindeer, I can, even if it has to be in secret. I can show Mikkal that I'm not on any 'side'. I want the truth. I know that's what Mum wants too, she's just intimidated by Andrei, they all are.

Mum strokes my hair. "Are you hungry, love? Shall we go over to the canteen?"

Leaving our building, we stop in surprise at the crowd of people outside. Town and Greenlight people alike.

Rolls of neon green light chase across the sky, forming and unforming. The horizon dances with it. A green sea in the sky, just like Pia said.

Mum squeezes my hand. "The *aurora borealis*," she whispers, and we chorus the words together, stretching out all the vowels. I tingle, thinking back to the plane journey.

Mum had made sure to give me the full scientific

explanation before we came out here. Blasts of electrified particles flare out from the sun and get trapped in our magnetic field, where they collide with gases to make explosions of light and colour. Green and red when they combine with oxygen; blue and purple when they combine with nitrogen.

Seeing it now, it doesn't just feel like light. It's more than that. It's some tremoring living thing blazing across the whole of the night sky.

I spot Mikkal in front of the canteen with Nina and the others. They look spellbound, even though they must have seen it hundreds of times before, all through their childhood.

Mum's arm drapes round me. "Did you know the Inuit people, in Alaska, believed the lights were the spirts of the animals they caught?" she tells me. "And in Finland, they thought it was a fire fox, running so fast his tail made bright sparks in the sky."

I look over to Mikkal again, where Kaiku's spinning around his feet as though the green lights have charged her with new energy.

I turn back to Mum. "In the book Dad gave me, it says Norse people thought the aurora were a rainbow bridge connecting the realm of the gods to the realm of mortals." I clasp the white whale in my pocket, thinking about Mikkal with two more brothers, and Nina's mum, never getting the chance to see her daughter grow up.

"That's a nice one to think about. A rainbow bridge," Mum breathes. I cuddle closer to her, and even though hunger grumbles through our stomachs, we watch the lights for ages.

# Hide and Seek

The children are running through the Cultural Palace, doors banging after them, cold air following in their wake. I'm on my frayed sofa under the grand staircase, picking at a loose thread of cushion.

A few days have passed now since the meeting and since Mikkal showed me the reindeer. Good as his word, he's kept his distance, and calls back Kaiku whenever she comes to say hello, though happily Kaiku isn't very good at obeying him.

So much for my plan to investigate the reindeer, however. The few I've seen seem strong and healthy and run away if I get too close, and Mum's started to shut me down if I ask too many questions. The stress of the job is getting to her.

"What's a corset?" I ask her now, coming up from the pages of the whaling book I've got open on my lap.

It holds a grim fascination for me. Maybe because bowheads live for hundreds of years, and they were killed in their tens of thousands. Numbers the seas are still missing all these years later.

"A corset?" Mum asks, surprised. She's decided to work beside me today. She's obviously feeling guilty about all the time I'm spending on my own. "They were a tight framed underwear. Women used to wear them, to pull in their waists. Why do you ask? You're not thinking of trying one?"

I roll my eyes theatrically, glad to hear Mum make a joke. I'm worried she's working too hard. Her cheeks have become pinched.

"That's what they used the baleen for, from the bowhead," I explain, flicking back to my favourite picture of the whale. Its mouth is open showing the hair-like structures spanning its top and bottom jaws. "They sold it for umbrellas and corsets and hoops for big skirts," I tell her.

"How horrible!" Mum shudders, and then says after a pause, "Isn't it amazing that whales are getting the chance to increase in numbers again? You know they're carbon sinks, like forests and peatlands. And like the permafrost here."

I nod. "Of course. We learned about it in primary." How when whales die, their gigantic bodies sink down to the bottom of the sea and all the carbon they've taken in during their long lives, stays locked away for hundreds of years. And whale poo, released in bursts as they come up to breathe, feeds carbon-absorbing plankton. Our teacher said that when our seas are full of whales again, we can worry less about climate change.

"You don't think the mine could be bad for the whales here?" I ask.

"For the whales?" Mum says, pursing her lips. "Not the methods we use, I've told you. We're not deep-sea drilling or anything like that."

"I know, but if the reindeer are getting sick, then what's to stop the whales getting sick too?"

"Rory," Mum coos gently. "Your mind's looking for problems. Honestly, trust me, we're not using anything dangerous. And stop picking at that thread, you'll pull it loose." Another blast of laughter and shouts come from upstairs and a few of the children tumble down the stairs and out into the square. Someone's always counting. It's a huge game of hide-and-seek that they resume every day.

I glance at the map spread open on Mum's knee. It's the island, with all the places the fjords cut into it, and the new mine site marked north west of here, along with other sites they're hoping to open up. The lines don't mean anything to me, but Mum scrutinizes them like she's deciphering ancient runes.

"Are you OK, Rory?" Mum asks, frowning at me now.

"I hope I didn't do the wrong thing, bringing you here."

"No, you didn't," I exclaim at once, anxious she'll start thinking about sending me back. "I like it here. Honestly, I do." It's no lie. Despite its remoteness and the plummeting temperature, despite the hostility of most of its people, it feels exactly right that I'm here. Even though I can't begin to explain why.

"Have you been sleeping OK?" Mum probes.

I nod uncomfortably, wishing I could move out of her glare.

"It must be lonely for you," Mum continues.

"I'm not lonely," I insist.

Mum's stare intensifies, and I give her an exaggerated smile. "I promise!" As if to make my point, Kaiku slips on to my lap. She must have got bored of the game they're all playing.

"See?" I say, smiling for real now, laying my hand on the fox's warm body.

Mum laughs affectionately. "You've always had a way with animals. It's a shame we're not allowed pets in the flat."

She goes back to her work and I doodle in the open page of my journal, where I've been attempting a picture of one of the bowheads. It's nothing like the ones on my wall. I'm sure that artist had seen them for real.

I look at some words that I wrote in the margins last

night, in tiny letters.

*Who are you?*

I'm not even sure who exactly I mean, I realize. The former inhabitant of my room, who left the whale drawings, or whoever I hear at night? Could they be the same person?

I angle the journal away from Mum. If she saw my scribbles she'd definitely start worrying about me.

Underneath the first, I write another question.

*What do you want?*

There's something about writing it down that focuses my mind on what it could all mean.

It's not just the noises. Last night I was sure I glimpsed that face again, in the mirror of my room, just as I went to brush my hair.

It was just a second, and it didn't feel scary, somehow. All the children here keep their distance, I'm not a novelty any more, but the girl in the mirror, she's interested in me. I can feel it.

Someone yells on the floor above us. They've been found, and then Nina and one of the younger girls tumble down the stairs. Nina catches my eye and takes care to narrow hers into slits.

# Song

A noise wakes me, but as soon as I try to focus in to listen, everything goes quiet. Except the dogs in their huts, howling out to the wilderness. I persuaded Mum to go and see the sick reindeer today, but it was too late. They'd died and Rasmos had burned their bodies. He said he didn't want the bears coming for them.

I lean over to switch on the lamp. Yellow light floods into the room and my clothes hanging over the chair make strange shadows on the floor. I need to talk to Mum about doing a load of laundry. Or find the laundry room and do it myself.

I turn to the whales on the wall, reflecting on what Mum said about whales being carbon sinks. They're as good for the planet as thousands of acres of forest, our teacher had said.

I start to drift off when I hear a noise again.

It's outside in the corridor. A girl's voice, singing. The same familiar song the children play on the piano, and Ivan whistled up by the mine. Sad and sorrowful, yet beautiful too.

I can't ignore it any longer. I have to work out who, or what, it is.

I take a deep breath and steel myself to open the door. The orange strip lighting flickers over the empty corridor, doors shut either side. Could there be someone in one of those rooms, hiding out of sight? Or is it a radio playing downstairs, in the rooms where those two mine engineers are? The window rattles behind me and I glance back into the room, trying to catch a glimpse of that face again.

There's nothing. Only the dark silhouette of the buildings of Pyramiden, and the rocky mountains above. I've started leaving the curtains open. The face that night must have been my own reflection, or my mind, filling in gaps. A ghost town doesn't mean *actual* ghosts, I tell myself. There are real, solid people living here, I'm bound to hear noises. Just like at home in our apartment block, there's the thrum of air conditioning and traffic on the streets outside. One of the neighbours playing a violin and a couple who are always arguing.

The light blinks by the stairs and there's a scuffling sound again. Are there still birds up there, late to start their migration to warmer temperatures? Even in the couple of weeks since we arrived, the temperature has plummeted right down as the days grow shorter.

There are definite footsteps now. Someone walking the floor above where Pia said I might find paint. I still haven't been up there.

I move hesitantly towards the steps, drawn on by the singing. A draught hangs in the stairway, strangely directionless, and the stairs creak as I walk up.

I clutch the banister with my right hand, my left holding my torch full beam ahead. The top floor isn't partitioned into rooms and corridor like the floors below, this is just one big space with a low ceiling. There's a stale smell of old musty things, dust and bird droppings. Is this why the children run through all the buildings of Pyramiden but leave this one alone?

I shine my torch into the corners of the room, over rusty ice skates, broken chairs, metal bedsteads. The cans of paint Pia told me about. Other things are shrouded in dustsheets.

"Rory!" a voice whispers, from over by the window. "Rory!" I don't wait a second longer. Hearing my name is a step too far, and I turn and run all the way back down, my heart hammering against my ribcage like a trapped bird. I go to Mum's door instinctively, but as I'm about to knock, something stops me.

The singing again, fainter now. So faint you can barely hear it, and yet it's there, somewhere inside this building. It isn't even that menacing, if I think about it, and when I crawl under the bed covers, my mind plays it like a lullaby, singing of whales and ice and forgotten places.

# Mountain

Mum's tight-lipped and preoccupied over breakfast. She swirls a spoonful of sugar into her coffee. I gaze at her with surprise – sugar in hot drinks is one of her pet hates. *It's so terrible for your teeth, Rory.*

It flashes into my head that perhaps Mum hears noises at night too, but doesn't want to frighten me. I try to think of a clever way to ask her about it, because maybe I can reassure her, when she opens her mouth to speak.

"The Arctic Council's visit has been brought forward. I have to finish my report a week early." She gives her coffee a fresh stir.

"Is that enough time?" I ask gingerly. "We've only been here a couple of weeks." *And I haven't found out anything more about the reindeer*, I think to myself.

Mum sighs, and runs her fingers through her hair.

The silvery threads have dulled since we came here. She smiles at me. "It is what it is. I'm getting Mark to help move my desk today. I'm going to work in one of the spare rooms in our corridor. I need some quiet – it's too noisy in the office."

"That's nice," I say, cheering up at the thought of having Mum nearby, and her having some space away from Andrei and Mark.

"Then I can work in the evenings," Mum adds. "Without worrying I'm too far from you. I've got to make progress on that report. You should be making a start on some school work."

"School work?" I repeat loudly, the words seeming out of place here.

Mum's face twitches. "Yes, school work, Rory. You remember what that is?"

I glance over to where the children are sat, bowls of porridge in front of them. Nina seems to be telling a story, and the others are leaning in with excited eyes. I told Mum yesterday that I wasn't lonely, but watching them together now, loneliness settles in my chest. Whatever I'm hearing, or imagining I'm hearing at night, it's not like having a real friend. Is that the best I can do – a made-up face in the mirror?

Outside in the square, I wander around the edges of the different buildings. There's another reindeer grazing off to the side of the old school. I jump down from the walkway, trying to be quiet so as not to scare it off.

It looks up but doesn't stop chewing.

Meeting its eyes really is like looking at some ancient primitive beast. It's strong and stocky against the ground.

I take a photo on my phone, making sure to give the reindeer a wide berth. I don't want it using hard-won energy reserves racing away from me. I've seen how fast they move.

I carry on walking, past the whirr of air vents high up on the wall of the Cultural Palace.

I spot Mum with Mark, by another set of sheds like the dog huts. They're taking out the skidoos. They must be going back up to the mine. Why didn't Mum tell me? I thought she was going to be coming to work in our building today. And why can't I go on a skidoo to see the new mine for once? Mum's always been proud to show me other projects she's worked on. The number of times I've stood in a hard hat feigning interest in foundation depths and ground conditions of new apartment blocks back home... The one time she's working somewhere more exciting, I'm confined indoors!

Suddenly I know what I'm going to do today. I'm going to walk up to the old mine again. I can return the whale figurine and see if I can spot any other mine sites where the reindeer might be getting sick.

Leaving town alone breaks all the rules, but I'll be right by the covered gallery the whole way, and by the time I'm up on the mountainside I'll have plenty of visibility for bears.

I walk over to the gallery before I can change my mind, all the while expecting to hear someone shouting my name to call me back. But I get to the tunnel entrance without anyone stopping me.

The wooden structure creaks ominously beneath my feet. It feels longer and darker walking up alone, and there are no gulls today. Have they finally left?

At the top, I stop to catch my breath. Pyramiden looks smaller from here, but as sparse and remote as ever. This is the only place Mikkal and Nina and the others have ever called home. I wonder what they'd think of our crowded apartment block, and the roads and shops nearby, with new buildings going up all the time. Despite the air of abandonment, it feels like the buildings here were made to last forever.

My eyes move to the dark water beyond the town. Mikkal said this is where Jonne and his friend used to watch for whales.

Something startles me, and I spin round to survey the grey landscape. It's quiet, empty. Except I know in that way you just know sometimes, that someone's watching me. Something.

Could the noises from Paris have followed me here?

Yet this feels different, all through my body. The noises at night have become almost companionable. Now the hairs stand up on the back of my neck, and my stomach is tight and hollowed out.

The gallery whines in the wind. I turn slowly on the spot, 360 degrees, scanning the horizon, all my senses on red alert.

There. By the crosses.

Like it's waiting for me.

*Gjelder hele Svalbard.*

A polar bear. *Ursus maritimus.* A sea bear, except this is just a few metres away, on the side of the mountain.

Yellower than you'd think it would be. And bigger, so much bigger.

Terror and awe curdle in my stomach. This is a hunter, the king of the ice, an apex predator, and I'm here alone without a rifle. I broke the town's main rule.

If I walk backwards, I can possibly make it into the covered passageway that leads down the mountain. The bear's claws could rip the gallery apart if they wanted, but it's stood all these years. Would I be safe in there? Safer than here, on the exposed mountainside, that's for sure.

My heartbeat reverberates around my body, blood pounding, pounding. Time stops still for a second.

If I run, I know as certainly as I know anything, that I'm done for.

I take the tiniest step backwards.

Then, as though I've set off some unexploded dynamite in the mountainside, there's a sharp crack. Gunfire. An orange blast of something at the corner of my vision.

The bear blunders away across the scree.

Mikkal emerges from the tunnel, a rifle in his hands. He's shaking, his face struck with terror. "Rory!" he shouts, aghast. "What are you doing up here?"

The rifle trembles in his hands. I wonder if he's ever shot it before.

"I just came for a walk, to see the view," I scramble. My legs are weak and I'm shaking. It's like all the air has been sucked out of my lungs.

"To see the view?!" Mikkal yells. "Have you gone out of your mind? To come here alone!"

"I wanted to help save the reindeer. I thought I might be able to spot the other site," I go on, trying to take away some of the horror in Mikkal's face.

"You think you'd see it just like that, after we've been looking for weeks? You think you know better?"

"No, no," I say miserably. "I just wanted to do something. And there was this, I wanted to return it."

I take the white figurine out of my pocket with trembling fingers.

"The beluga?" Mikkal asks, still staring at me in horror and disbelief.

He rips it from my gloved hand and hurls it down the mountain. "If that bear hadn't run away, you do know the next thing I'd have had to do, don't you? You do know I'd have had to shoot her?"

"Don't!" I cry, tears smarting my eyes.

"She might have cubs somewhere!"

"No, Mikkal!" I plead. I don't want to hear any of it. I'm all too aware of what might have been. How neither of us might be standing here now. Or there'd be a dead polar bear at our feet. What was it that Pia had said that first night about everyone having to think about their actions here? It's kill or be killed.

"She was about to attack, Rory! No joke! A second later and she would have been on you. *You* would have been dead, Rory!"

Tears roll down my cheeks properly now. Mikkal starts stomping off down the tunnel in disgust. A storm of fear, shock and humiliation churns around inside me.

"Will you tell everyone?" I ask, following him down the gallery, imagining everyone's reactions when they hear. Mum angry and afraid, refusing to let me outside here ever again. Andrei and Mark probably wishing I had been eaten, if they could only hush it up for the Arctic Council. Pia's disappointment at my recklessness. The scorn in Nina's restless eyes.

Mikkal turns back, his face lit by a crack in the wooden

casing. "We always report bear sightings close to town."

"But will you tell them I was up here? Alone? My mum…" I sob, overcome at the thought of Mum finding out.

Would she send me home? Would she summon the *Leviathan* and send me back alone? Or worse, be consumed with parental obligation and feel she had to accompany me, in which case her Arctic adventure would be over too. She'd return in a cloud of shame, her reputation ruined by her errant daughter, and the future of this place left in Andrei's hands.

Mikkal pauses for a few seconds before shaking his head slowly. "I'll keep your secret. If you promise never to do that again. Never, ever." He pats his chest, and I know his heart is hammering just as strongly as mine.

"Never, ever," I say, holding his gaze. "I won't forget it."

# Satellite

"Could he be out?" the engineer says, fiddling with the wires for the satellite phone. "There's no answer."

I'm still trembling after the encounter with the bear and desperate to speak with someone friendly. Mum's not back yet.

"Maybe," I say, glancing at my watch, calculating the time difference back to the UK. Dad doesn't have much of a routine. He can be out at any time of day or night. He might be checking the moth traps or seeing how the bats are doing in the empty barn a few minutes' walk from the cabin. "I'll keep trying." I wipe a fresh tear from my eye, and the man looks away embarrassed. I recognize him from our building. He's one of the people staying on the ground floor.

"Your father will pick up soon, I hope," he says in his

Norwegian accent.

I nod, and swallow back my tears. "Thank you. You don't need to wait," I assure him. "He won't be out long."

The man disappears down the corridor, and I slump on to the floor. I won't be able to tell Dad about the bear. Today grinds inside me, raw and shameful, but if I can at least hear his voice... Sometimes Dad makes me feel better without saying very much at all.

I continue to dial the number, listening to the buzzing tone at the other end. I have no idea if that means it's engaged or not connecting.

"It won't work like that," a voice says. I start. Nina is standing in the doorway, watching me.

"He told me it would," I say stubbornly. "One of the engineers. He did something to it." I rub at my blotchy cheeks and turn away from her. She's the last person I want to see right now.

"Who did you want to talk to?" Nina asks, not moving from her spot.

"It doesn't matter," I say, stabbing Dad's number back into the metal contraption, to be met with the same lifeless tone.

"Whatever he did, it's not working," Nina insists.

I stare at the device in my hand hopelessly.

"I could get my dad to look at it. If you want me to."

I glance at Nina suspiciously, wondering if it's a trick.

"I just wanted to speak with my dad," I murmur. "It doesn't matter."

Nina stares back at me for a moment, and then turns around. "Wait here," she orders over her shoulder, already disappearing around the corner.

I pace the corridor, peering through the glass wall into the main Greenlight office. The door's locked. On one of the desks, Mum's things are packed into a box, ready to be carried across to our building. Once she's working there, I should have a better chance of looking at all the maps and diagrams, and maybe Mum'll be more receptive to questions about what could be making the reindeer sick. There must be a way I can help uncover the truth about what's happening here.

Ivan appears in the corridor as silently as his daughter did, and bends straight away to the discarded phone. "The wires are loose," he pronounces after a few seconds.

He takes out a screwdriver from his pocket and starts fiddling with odd screws and connections. "They should have asked me in the beginning. This phone has been our only link to the mainland."

I nod shyly.

"You OK?" Ivan asks, scrutinizing my face. "You look like you've seen a ghost!"

"I'm fine," I splutter, my cheeks reddening, afraid Mikkal has said something after all, about the bear. He might have felt it was his duty.

Ivan hands me the phone – "It'll work now" – and strides away before I can say a proper thank you. I crouch back down to floor level. Even though the office is empty, I want to be out of its glare to make the call.

Dad answers at once, his voice calm and familiar. "Rory! Kiddo! How are you?"

I nod furiously, struggling to regain my composure, and then realize of course that head movements don't translate across regular phone lines, never mind a call that beams my voice to an orbiting satellite, and back down to the UK phone network.

"Rory?" Dad checks. "You there, kiddo?"

I laugh with relief. "I'm good, Dad."

"Is there snow?" he asks excitedly.

"Yes, yes!" I say, brighter now. "But everyone says this is just a scattering and there will be more soon. Much deeper."

"And have you seen any wildlife yet?"

"Of course!" I chatter on, telling Dad about the boat trip over here, and the seals and the walrus, and then I enthuse about Kaiku, how she's silvery blue, like moonlight. "And she really likes me, Dad! She's always jumping on to my knee to nap."

"Ah, Rory, you sound so alive! It's wonderful! What an adventure you're having. Have you seen reindeer too?"

"Yes, them too," I say instantly, then pause.

"And what are they like?" Dad enquires, as if sensing something unsaid.

"Beautiful, except some are sick. The children here—"

"The children?" Dad interrupts, and I realize I've forgotten to mention the biggest surprise about this place, and I go off on a tangent telling him about Mikkal and Nina and the others.

"What was it you were saying about these sick reindeer?" Dad asks after a while, pulling me back to the topic. I'm aware of a crushing feeling around my heart as I recall the trembling, dying creatures Rasmos had in the shed, and Mikkal's insistence that Greenlight, Mum's company, is somehow responsible.

"The townspeople think it's to do with the rare earth mining," I mutter.

"And what does your mum say?" Dad asks.

"Mum's just busy," I answer, my voice quieter now. "She doesn't have that much time to talk to me. But she says the sick reindeer aren't related to the mining."

"What do you think?" Dad continues. I can hear faint sounds of the cabin. A crackling fire, an owl hooting. "Come on, kiddo," Dad urges. "You've got a clever head on you. I bet you've got an opinion?"

I laugh hollowly, acutely aware now of all the things this conversation has skipped over. The noises in our building

163

at night. How the children aren't meant to talk to me – that it's a ghost town, but it's me that feels like the ghost here sometimes. The paranoid atmosphere among the Greenlight people. The days getting shorter as the polar night moves ever closer.

"I don't know, Dad," I venture, holding the phone up and shaking it a little, realizing how empty the line sounds. "Dad? Are you there?" I extend out the antennae and stand on my tiptoes but the signal is well and truly dead. Maybe just as well, I find myself thinking, because I still don't have a clue how I'd answer that last question.

# Forest

It's the day after the bear encounter. Mikkal spots me on my usual sofa, my journal open on the table, and heads over. I look up, surprised. Has he forgotten his anger yesterday?

"What are you doing?" he asks, looking down with interest at the open book.

I shut it quickly. Showing him my midnight scribbles is not a good way to make friends.

"It's a sort of diary," I say tentatively, yesterday all too fresh in my memory. "To help me remember this place. And to show my dad. When I'm home."

"Your dad didn't want to come out here?" Mikkal asks, taking a seat beside me.

"He had to stay behind. To work. He lives in a forest," I tell him.

"A forest!" Mikkal's ears prick up. It strikes me that he'll never have seen one. He won't even have seen a tree.

I scroll back through my phone gallery. Almost all my photos before coming here, I realize, were taken in the forest. Leaves, light, shadows. Crows, magpies, jays. I've taken photos of spiderwebs and patterns of bark. Moss and lichens. Weird fungus forms.

Mikkal stares at them mesmerized, and I press the phone into his hand so he can look closer. I show him how to move back and forth between the different images.

"You're lucky," he murmurs, still engrossed in the pictures. "To live in the trees."

I frown, wondering how to explain the two sides of my life when I'm so far away from both of them. "I don't live in the forest all the time. Most of the time I live with my mum, in a town. Bigger than this one. It's where I go to school."

I look through the window to the abandoned school building, wondering how much Mikkal even knows about school.

"My dad used to live with us too, in town, but he was never really happy. He said there wasn't enough air to breathe and he couldn't see the stars." I pause, and then speak in a rush. "Sometimes I feel that too. But not here."

Mikkal grins. "We don't have that problem in our town."

"No," I say in agreement. "My dad would like it here."

"So you are part town and part forest?" Mikkal says.

I shrug. "I don't know what I am. I'm just me." After a pause I ask, "Why did so many people stay here, after the mine accident?"

"There wasn't anywhere to go," Mikkal says. "This was home, and the places where everyone had come from – since the Global Climate Act, those places had changed. The housing we were offered, it wasn't good…" He screws his face up. "Though maybe it would have been better." He reaches out to stroke the blue folds of Kaiku's fur. "She's good to have around when you're sad," he says, smiling at me.

"I'm not sad," I say quietly. "Just shaken, and ashamed." My eyes flit upwards, recalling our recent proximity to the bear.

Mikkal puts his finger to his lips. "I thought we weren't talking about it here."

I nod gratefully. "Where did your family come from?" I ask him, keen to make sense of this boy, who forgives so easily and talks so openly.

"We were born and brought up here, Jonne and I," Mikkal says lightly. "But my parents, originally, were Sami."

"Sami?" I ask, unsure.

"Sami people were nomadic. My parents lived in the northern part of Finland. They moved with the reindeer.

But it's in the Wilderness Zone now. Everyone was moved away."

Mikkal plucks at the sofa like I do, a melancholic look on his face now. "That's why some of them came here. Mum said it was either come here or go and live in some housing project in Helsinki, far away from the lands they'd grown up in. So even though they were against mining, this is where they ended up. In Pyramiden."

"They were against mining?" I question, interested. "Because of climate change?"

"Yes," Mikkal concedes, "and because it was disturbing the earth. Mum thinks the accidents were punishment for that. She misses their old lands. One day I'll go back with her. We'll live in the forests again, with the reindeer."

He looks up at me fiercely, as if expecting me to contradict what he's saying.

I smile. "That sounds nice. It would be a change from here."

Mikkal laughs, and then stands suddenly. "You have to come with me, Rory." He holds out his hand to pull me up.

"What do you mean?" I ask uncertainly.

"My mum should see your forest pictures. You have to come back and meet her. At my home."

My face bends quizzically at his unexpected invitation. What would the rest of the townspeople make of that?

"My mum would love it," Mikkal insists. "She's been saying we should include you more in our games. Please come. It's safer than the mountain, I promise!"

# Fossils

Mikkal pushes me on through the hallway of his apartment block and opens a door two thirds of the way down the corridor. The room inside smells of cooking and my stomach growls in response to it.

"*Eadni!*" Mikkal calls.

Mikkal's mum emerges in a doorway off the main room and smiles at me with obvious surprise, wiping her hands on her apron. "Rory, isn't it? How are you finding our old town?"

I smile shyly, keen to make a good impression. "It's beautiful and, well, like nowhere else, I suppose. I like it. A lot."

Mikkal's mum pulls a chair out from under a sturdy table and bids me to sit. Kaiku's asleep on a softer armchair, I notice. She's lost in some dream and her legs tremble as if she's running.

"Heat up some water," Mikkal's mum says, ruffling her son's hair. "You can make hot chocolate while I talk to your new friend. I don't get to meet many new people here. I'm Inger-Mari. I've heard much about you from my son."

Mikkal disappears into the kitchen and the sound of a metal pan clanking floats out after him.

My fingers stray towards a bowl of white-grey substance in the centre of the table. Like dandelion seeds, interwoven with little flecks of moss. Strands dance into the air like threads of moonlight.

"It's eider down," Mikkal's mum tells me, smiling.

"From the ducks?" I ask, trying not to show disapproval. I know it's different out here. People have to use the resources available. Like eating the fish or hunting reindeer.

"Calm down, animal saviour," Mikkal teases, appearing in the doorway. "The birds that lost these feathers will still be swimming on the fjords."

Mikkal's mum nods. "The mothers pluck out feathers from their own bodies to lay around their eggs to keep them warm."

"Doesn't that hurt?" I blurt out.

"You underestimate a mother's devotion, Rory," Mikkal's mum says laughing. "We collect it from their nests after the ducklings have been born. We use it for pillows and blankets. This will go into a new cover for Mikkal's bed."

There's a slosh of water boiling in the little kitchen, and Mikkal turns back into the space, his mum flying after him, tutting good-naturedly at his lack of concentration.

I stand to examine a shelf winding round the room like a wave. It looks to be made of driftwood and on it are copper-coloured rocks with leaf imprints that I peer at curiously.

"Fossils," Mikkal says behind me now, making me jump. His mum must have discharged him from the kitchen. "My dad found them in the mines."

I pull back my hand.

Mikkal laughs. "Don't worry. They've survived millions of years already. You won't damage them."

Something I read before my trip comes back to me, that Svalbard was once on the equator and was hot and tropical.

I get a stab of longing for different circumstances, where Mum could come here too and talk at length about these millions-of-years-old patterns of life forms.

My eye's caught by a line of whale figurines further along the shelf, just like the one I found at the mine entrance. I could name them all from the pictures on my bedroom wall. Narwhal, minke, beluga, bowhead, orca, humpback, and then the two biggest whales on Earth: the blue and the fin whale.

"Mikkal told me you found one of my son's models?" Mikkal's mum says, coming back into the room with mugs of steaming liquid.

I nod, awkwardly, hoping she doesn't ask to see it. That beluga is lost on the mountainside now.

She smiles. "Jonne leaves them all over the island. Mikkal must have told you they're for his childhood friend?" She places the mugs down on the table. They chime together softly. "Ulya, she was called. She loved the whales here."

I run my fingers through my hair uncomfortably. "I'm sorry. About everything that happened."

"You don't need to be sorry, Rory," Mikkal's mum says tranquilly. "It was before your time. Mikkal was just a baby then. Look."

She holds up a photo from the shelf. She's hand in hand with a bearded man. They're both fit and happy, standing proudly next to their three tall boys, plus the baby, Mikkal, in his dad's arms. He looks cute and podgy and is reaching for the camera.

There's a moment's silence as we stare at the photo. The three lives lost, who should be here now, stretching out their legs at the table, or helping Mikkal's mum keep the family warm and fed.

"But life moves on," Mikkal's mum says with a resigned sigh, pulling at the strings of her apron. "Especially for you young people. That's important."

She beckons me to drink, and I show her photos of

Dad's woodland on my phone. Mikkal proudly demonstrates that he knows how to scroll. There's a look of sadness in Inger-Mari's eyes as she gazes at them, and I move over to Kaiku, to stroke her dreaming form.

"I have soup warming on the stove too. I shall get you both bowls," Mikkal's mum says suddenly, getting up to make her way back over to the kitchen. It's just a few footsteps away in the small apartment.

"No," Mikkal says springing to his feet, his face flushed. "Rory can't stay for lunch. Can you?" he says, looking at me deliberately.

I shake my head uncertainly. "I could, I think. It smells nice whatever—"

"You won't think it's nice," Mikkal says.

Mikkal's mum looks on sternly. "What do you mean, Mikkal? Are you ashamed of my cooking?"

"I'm not ashamed, Mum. But Rory won't want it. She doesn't eat it."

"Eat what?" I ask, baffled by the way he's acting.

"Reindeer," he says awkwardly.

The smell makes sense now. My eyes move to the floor – a reindeer hide by the fire and another on a soft chair.

"I... I..." The words stick in my mouth.

"You see," says Mikkal, an edge of bitterness in his voice.

A new draught of air blows in as the door to the apartment opens. "What's she doing here?" a voice says in

174

the doorway. Jonne. "Why did you bring her?"

Mikkal's mum goes to take his coat, tutting. "Shush, Jonne. That's not how we treat guests."

"How do we know she's not a spy, come to seek information from us?"

Mikkal's brow furrows. "Rory wouldn't do that!"

"If my mum thought the mine was damaging anything, she wouldn't be involved in it," I say defensively. "I know her. And Pia too."

Jonne's expression changes at Pia's name. "Pia makes her own choices."

"Now, Jonne," Mikkal's mum interjects. I can feel Mikkal squirming uncomfortably beside me. "Leave Rory be. It's nice for Mikkal to have a new friend round."

I smile gratefully at her. "All the same, I think I ought to go now. My mum... She might be worried." The magic of the eider down and the whales on the shelf is broken.

"It's not that I disapprove of you having reindeer meat," I tell Mikkal awkwardly, in the hallway now, struggling to put on my boots before I stumble out into the cold. "I see why you would, eat them I mean."

"No, you don't," Mikkal replies quietly. "You think it's wrong. You think you never would eat it."

I stare back at him, knowing he's speaking the truth. "But that doesn't mean we can't be friends, does it?"

Mikkal pauses for a moment. Mikkal's mum comes up

behind him and pushes him. "Of course it doesn't, Rory. Of course you should be friends."

Kaiku circles round my feet, yipping as though in agreement.

"Thank you for having me," I say politely. "I think your home is lovely, and I would have tried the soup, it's just…" I pause, "It's different where I come from."

Mikkal's mum puts her hands gently on Mikkal's shoulders. "We understand, Rory. Thank you for coming over. I hope to see you again before you leave."

# Daytrip

I wake late, though outside it's pitch black. The sun's not rising till late morning now.

Pia's cleared her schedule to take me and Mum to the glacier today. In a couple of hours we'll be standing on the ice with an actual glaciologist!

It'll be good to spend time with Mum too. It feels as if I haven't talked to her properly for days.

I pull on layers of clothes – tights beneath leggings beneath the thick cords Mum bought me ready for our trip, and four separate tops under my sweater.

Mum's not in her room, nor in the bathroom across the hallway. The pipes are gurgling, however, so I figure she must just have gone down for breakfast.

I spy her at once as I enter the canteen. She's at a table with a couple of the engineers, and Mark, their heads bent over some papers.

Mum must feel my eyes on her because she sits up and looks right at me. She gets up to walk over.

"You looked so grown up there for a moment," she says, giving me a quick hug. "Did you sleep better last night?"

"You've had breakfast already? You should have woken me!" I say, ignoring her question and looking at her suspiciously.

There's an awkward silence. Mum's eyes flicker.

"You can't come to the glacier, can you?" I say.

Mum gives a reluctant sigh. "Oh, Rory. A new site can be so tricky in the beginning. All these things we hadn't anticipated, and a new team, everyone finding their feet..."

"But you promised, Mum!" I cry, not wanting to hear her excuses.

"Perhaps I can finish early, another day this week, or next week some time..."

"You promised," I say again, louder now. Mikkal, Nina and the others are at a nearby table eating breakfast and their faces turn towards me.

"I could ask one of them to come," I say to Mum deliberately.

Mum frowns. "Oh, I think the glacier trip's off. I'd feel nervous about you going without me, and Pia has to work on her report. We're running out of time for the investors. Andrei is worried they'll lose interest."

Just at that moment Pia swings by, two mugs of coffee in her hands. She must have been at the serving hatch already.

"Twenty minutes OK, Rory? Meet you in the entrance to the Cultural Palace? We can walk to the boat together. I'm sorry you can't make it, Laura. But at least Rory will still get to see it. Jonne is going to come across with us."

I can't help but give Mum a triumphant look that the outing is still on. Then I turn to Pia. "Does Jonne know I'm coming?" I ask, nervous after yesterday's obvious hostility at finding me in his home.

"Of course. He's going to defend us against polar bears!" Pia says happily. She's in a good mood, like it's a holiday. Her hair's tied back in pigtails and she's wearing tiny turquoise earrings in the shape of snowflakes.

"Please come, Mum!" I say, pulling at her arm. She deserves a day off too. She's been working non-stop since we arrived, and it's not even really a day off. Mum's always on about the importance of thinking about the whole of a site. Svalbard wouldn't make sense without its glaciers.

"I'm sorry, Rory, it's impossible," Mum says with another sigh.

"Well, I'm still coming," I say, addressing Pia directly now.

Mum puts her hand up. "Hang on a minute, Rory. That's not your decision to make." She leans in to Pia. "What do you know about this Jonne?"

Pia laughs and replies at full volume. I see some of the Greenlight staff looking our way too now. "I know Jonne's the best boatsman around here. He knows the glacier much better than me."

Mum crinkles her face. "I'm just not sure. Rory's inexperienced here, in this kind of landscape. It's such an inhospitable place."

"Mum!" I cry in frustration. "I've been so excited about going. You know I have!"

"I suppose if you stay close to Pia…"

"Mum!" I cringe, giving Pia a look of apology. She's not here to be my babysitter – she's a scientist.

Mum's jaw hangs open for a few seconds deliberating, then the Greenlight people start getting up, scraping their chairs along the floor, and Mum looks over anxiously, not wanting to be left behind. She gives me another quick hug, issues Pia a plea to look after me, and turns to leave. "Take some photos," she calls back over her shoulder.

Mikkal summons me over after they've gone. "Come and sit with the young people, Rory!" he sings, and the others budge up to make space for me. Even Nina throws me a faint smile. I think about thanking her for getting her dad to fix the phone, but I have a feeling she won't want the others to know she helped me.

"You'd better eat quickly if we're visiting the glacier, Rory!" Mikkal says brightly.

I look at him, surprised. "We?"

Mikkal smiles. "There's no way I'm being left behind. Kaiku loves being on the boat. You should see her, looking over the side for eider ducks. We have to be careful she doesn't jump in!"

I hug my arms together with pleasure, extra happy at the prospect of spending a day with them both.

"The glacier is too cold and far now for me," Nina moans, pulling a face and shivering her shoulders. "The ice is coming in. Watch, any day now."

"But not today," Mikkal declares, meeting my gaze and winking. "This is Rory's once-in-a-lifetime adventure. She must see the glacier while she is here."

# Glacier

Mikkal leaps across on to the boat. "You almost left without me!"

Kaiku bounds after him effortlessly, and noses into my side.

"Hi, Mikkal!" Pia calls, smiling as Kaiku moves on to her with her exuberant nudges. "I was hoping you would both join us."

"Someone needs to check Rory doesn't get eaten by bears!" Mikkal exclaims. "What would Greenlight think to that?"

I give him a playful push. "Do you think we'll see bears today?"

"They are unpredictable." Mikkal waves his arm over the vast expanse. "But there's always a chance here. This is a wilderness, you know!"

Pia has moved to the front of the boat with Jonne. They're deep in conversation, easy in each other's company.

Mikkal and I are too, any residual awkwardness slipping away as we get further from the town, sailing over the dark water.

"How were the ice mice last night?" he asks conversationally.

"Maybe it's all in my head," I say with a shiver. "That's what Mum says. She says it's this place, the old buildings and the dark…"

"But that's not what you think?"

I hold his gaze for a moment, wondering how much I should tell him. "Sometimes I hear footsteps, outside in the corridor, and above in the attic. A child, I think. A girl."

The lines above Mikkal's eyebrows crease. "One of the town kids? Nina, up to her tricks? I'll talk with her. I'm surprised she went up alone. She's genuinely scared of that building."

I shake my head quickly. "I don't think it was Nina."

"Buppha and Nan? Those girls get everywhere!"

"No," I start, but when I think how impossible any other explanation is I stop. "Maybe. Maybe it was them, or one of the others. I thought they were trying to play tricks on me in the beginning, to scare me. But it doesn't feel like that any more. It feels almost … friendly."

Mikkal stares at me strangely.

"Anyway," I say firmly. "Today's going to be about real people. And a real fox," I add, as Kaiku curls up in my lap.

Mikkal nods his head in agreement. "Only bears and ice today, yes?"

I smile. "Ice and a bear from a far, far distance, maybe."

Mikkal laughs and I feel warm inside that we have a shared secret, even if the memory of it makes me recoil in shame.

The closer we get to the glacier, the more ice there is in the water. We pass a tall iceberg and Mikkal and I hang over the guardrail. If we were any closer, we could reach out and touch it.

"The glacier is calving," Pia explains, leaving Jonne at the tiller to stand next to us. "Parts of it are breaking away."

"What will happen to the iceberg now?" I ask.

"This one will probably drift south and melt," Pia says.

I snap a photo with my phone, imagining the ancient blue chunk of ice melting into the sea. We might be the last people to ever look at it.

"We have to hope the world woke up in time. We have to hope this place will survive. Either way, we're lucky we get to see it." Pia touches my shoulder.

I nod intently. We're much closer to the edge of the glacier now. It's high and steep, and blue waterfalls cascade down from the side in a couple of places. There's a lower section where the glacier slants down into the fjord, and this is where we're obviously heading. Pia shows us how to strap crampons – frames of metal spikes – to the underside of our boots.

"You'll need these too," she says, handing both Mikkal and me an ice axe. "To steady yourself if you start to fall."

"Will it be dangerous?" I ask, looking at my axe and then back to the icy landscape we're about to explore.

Pia smiles. "We've picked our landing place carefully. It's one of the flatter places, without too many crevasses."

Jonne takes the boat in as close as he can get to the edge of the glacier, before throwing down an anchor. We basically have to jump over the gap and hope for the best. My heart drops as my feet leave the relative safety of the boat, but I manage to scramble on to the ice, the spikes of the crampons giving a satisfying crunch as they land. I look around with exhilaration. Wait till I tell Dad about this!

I stick close to Pia as we learn how to traverse the ice. Nothing feels very solid and we have to walk with our feet apart, like penguins, because of the crampons over our boots.

Kaiku in contrast slips around helplessly, and Pia and Jonne double over laughing at her.

"She's too small," Mikkal says defensively, scooping her up.

Pia laughs. "I reckon she knows how to manage this

landscape better than any of us."

"I'm not having her falling down a crevasse," Mikkal insists.

Just as he speaks, an unearthly moan sounds below us.

If it wasn't for my crampons' grip on the ice, I'd have jumped a couple of metres in the air. "Is that normal?" I cry.

Pia smiles. "It's air, moving in the ice. You get used to it. The ice is talking to us. Part of my job is to learn its language."

"What's it saying today?" Jonne asks, stopping to stare at her.

Pia brushes her hair back from her face and crouches down, her head tilted to the ice playfully. She's silent for a few moments, then she smiles. "It's saying welcome to Rory. It's saying what an honour it is to have her here."

I laugh and give a pretend bow to the ice while Jonne rolls his eyes, though he's different today. More at ease. We're all so much more relaxed away from the town.

"Why's the ice blue?" Mikkal asks. "Shouldn't ice be clear, or white?"

"Not when it's so tightly packed," Pia answers. "The pressure forces out the air bubbles – that's some of the sounds you're hearing – and the change in structure means it absorbs light differently. Much more red light is absorbed than blue, and so here you have it. So blue that it's turquoise."

Pia gazes across the peaks and troughs of the crystalline landscape.

Mikkal nudges me, and tilts his head towards his brother, who's watching Pia adoringly, his pale cheeks flushed red. I take a quick photo of them and then move on to nimble-footed Kaiku, who's back down on the ice. The blue fox against the blue glacier. It's like seeing her in her own queendom.

"Will you take a photo of me?" I say to Mikkal shyly. "So I can show my dad that we came here?"

"That's a great idea!" Pia exclaims, overhearing. "Stand with Mikkal, Rory. I'll take one of both of you."

Mikkal and I hold our ice axes in the air like Vikings, with Kaiku between us, tail in the air like she's posing too. Mikkal and I roar into the camera. Even though my nose is numb and my fingers burn with cold, I'm happier than I've been in ages.

# Blubbertown

"One more stop," Jonne announces, as he restarts the boat's engine, his eyes fixed on the flowers of ice in the dark water.

Mikkal and Pia exchange glances.

"Jonne!" Pia complains. "We're cold already. Think of our fingers and toes!"

"We're so near. We should see it," Jonne says brusquely.

"See what?" I ask uneasily, sensing something between them all.

"You'll find out," Jonne answers.

I try to catch Mikkal's gaze, but he looks away, stroking Kaiku who's flopped with exhaustion on his lap. A flame of unease lights up in my stomach.

"It's fine, Rory," Pia says with a reassuring smile. "I'll make sure we're back before dark."

We steer into the next bay along, where the floes of ice look newly formed. The fjord starting to freeze over for its winter sleep.

The hull grinds against the rocks at the bottom as Jonne brings the boat in closer to the sloping shore. "Too close!" Mikkal snaps, but his brother shakes his head undeterred and throws the anchor down into the water. The rope barely unravels. We're in the shallows.

"What is this place?" I ask, standing up to get a better view. It looks oddly familiar. Mounds of earth and rock are set back from the shore in strange patterns. A page of photos from that whaling book flashes into my head.

"It's one of the old whaling stations, isn't it?" I say. Jonne makes a sudden leap over the remaining section of ice and water.

"No, Jonne!" Pia says more urgently now. "Don't get off. We need to get Rory and Mikkal back. It'll get late. Laura will be worried. She trusted me."

Jonne ignores her and beckons for me to follow him off the boat.

"Jonne!" Pia cries in frustration but I nod my head, looking back at Mikkal and Kaiku still curled up on his lap before making my own jump to shore. My feet skid on the rocks and ice, but Jonne's hands are ready and he keeps me upright.

Pia and Mikkal reluctantly make their way across too

and newly awake Kaiku follows though she stays close to our feet. Perhaps she's tired after her glacier adventure.

It's a different landscape again here. There are silvery logs on the beach and Mikkal bends down and runs his hand against one of their edges. The rings of the tree are laid out like concentric moons. "Sliced, you see. They escaped one of the timber farms, in Siberia, maybe."

I trace the growth rings in the log, walking my gloved fingers through the years, picturing its flight down an icy river and its plunge into the Arctic Ocean. So Mikkal has seen a tree after all, though these ones are long dead. Ghost trees. "How long ago do you think it was felled?" I ask him. "It looks ancient."

Mikkal nods his head. "Some of the logs will have been trapped in the sea ice for centuries. Then the ice melts and they end up here. There's not much to make things decay in Svalbard."

The shore is moon crater-like, strewn with the driftwood and the ghost trees.

Jonne and Pia have moved further up the beach and are standing over something.

"A reindeer," Mikkal breathes, running towards them. I follow, a sinking feeling in my stomach.

The reindeer's dead. Jonne catches my eyes as I approach.

"What will happen to it?" I ask, grimacing at the hollowed form of the poor creature. Its gums are blackened and its teeth yellow and crooked.

"A bear will come for it," Jonne tells me. "Or it'll wash into the sea for a whale."

"But that's not safe, is it?" I cry. "Whatever poisoned it, it will spread out."

Jonne nods sombrely. "You see why it's important we stop this."

I swallow, and stare over his shoulder where I see two white shapes in the water. A yelp catches in my throat. They're belugas. The white Arctic whales! Like the little carved one I found at the mine opening.

I turn back to Jonne, the top of my head tingling. Real-life whales. It's like he conjured them up for me. "They are always here in this bay," he says, shrugging. "It's like they remember. Even the bowheads come. I used to watch for them here…"

I see Pia glance at him oddly, her eyebrows furrowed.

"I read about this place," I say quietly, recalling the scenes from the book. The fjords frothing with whales, spouting blood, thrashing for their lives. I walk to the edge of the water.

Jonne nods as if he can see what's in my head. "A hundred years after the whalers came, there was no point even sending the ships. All the whales had gone. So the trappers came instead. For polar bears, seals, walrus, foxes." My eyes travel to the sleek form of Kaiku, silvery in the dimming light. Jonne swallows. "This is what I was trying to get everyone to understand at your mum's meeting!"

"Jonne!" Pia interrupts softly. "Rory doesn't need to hear all this. The past is the past."

Jonne wrings out his hands. "Someone has to listen! Perhaps a child understands better than any of us. These are the creatures this island belongs to, and now your people come here again, to take elements right out of the earth."

Pia winces and looks away to where the grey scree slips into the water. I swallow uncomfortably. *Your* people. It's hardly fair. Anyone who saw Pia on that glacier would know how important this place is to her.

"Are you going to ask her then?" Mikkal says, not looking up at me. He's twirling his right foot in the grey rocks.

"Ask me what?" I say.

No one says anything for a moment, there's just the sound of waves on the shore and ice clacking against the rocks.

After a while it's Pia who speaks. "The extraction isn't happening the way Greenlight thought it would, Rory," she tells me, her eyes meeting Jonne's. "It's too cold for the bacteria they were using to separate out the rare earths. Especially now, as the temperature drops. We think that instead they're using acids and chemicals. Andrei is desperate, his whole project is going to fail unless they use them, even though they know if the Arctic

Council finds out they would never get their approval. So they're covering it up. Lying."

"They can't be!" I cry. "Mum said—"

"Your mum doesn't know," Pia says gently but forcefully, her eyes on mine now. "Or at least she doesn't know everything." She hesitates. "The townspeople have been looking for evidence but Greenlight must have been doing it at another site. We think there's a tailings pond somewhere, with poisonous waste materials. Jonne and Ivan have been trying to find it, but Andrei and Mark and the others are good at covering their tracks. They go off secretly on their skidoos, and then the snow comes and it's impossible to find out where it's happening. But we think that's what's been making the reindeer sick."

I get a rush of foreboding.

Mikkal breathes in sharply. "We need recent maps of the sites they're using."

"But don't you have them?" I look at Pia, confused. "You work for Greenlight."

Pia laughs bitterly. "Have you not noticed, Rory? How they look at me? Whisper about me? The moment I became friends..." She pauses as she says this last word. "When Jonne and I became friends, Andrei and Mark didn't like it. I barely have access to anything now. Even Ingrid is annoyed with me, she thinks I turned 'traitor'."

"Why can't we just ask my mum about it? I'll ask her

if you don't want to—"

Jonne interrupts angrily. "That would ruin everything. Your mum is one of them."

Pia looks at me sadly. I'm about to protest Mum's innocence to them all, but that horrible meeting comes back to me. Mum at the podium defending Greenlight, and all the days recently, going off in the skidoo with Mark to the mine. Is Mum one of them now?

"There must be plans outlining where all their operations have been," Jonne continues. "The tailings pond with the chemicals, it must be somewhere the reindeer go to graze. We've been looking everywhere but we're running out of time. We've tried following them but they have their skidoos, and we're not so silent with the dogs, and on foot it's impossible, the distances are vast, the terrain difficult."

I listen carefully. Haven't I been wanting to help? And I know it would help Mum too, in the end. She doesn't want to sign off a project that could damage this place forever.

"We need evidence to show the Arctic Council when they come back," Jonne says. "There is much money in the Svalbard project for them. But if we have evidence that the wildlife in their precious wilderness is being damaged, then they cannot be seen to ignore it. If we could get hold of more of their maps. If *you* could, Rory." His eyes bore into me.

Mikkal's still twirling his foot in the scree.

"I'll try," I gulp, glancing between them, keen for their approval. "Mum's moved her desk to Building Nine, to Paris. To be near me. If she has access to any other maps, I'll find them for you."

There's a creak from the glacier and all of us turn back to look at it. The belugas are still swimming in the bay and another iceberg is calving out into the fjord. *What's the glacier saying now?* I wonder. Surely it would agree I should help them? The animals here can't be put at risk again.

Jonne points to a circle of light around the moon. "We should get back. Snow is coming."

# Deception

I pause outside Mum's new office. Someone's in there with her. Mark. Unease crawls into my stomach at the thought of that horrible man in our corridor.

My ears prick up.

*Rory.* They're talking about me. I stand silently behind the door, peering through the crack.

Mum's sighing loudly. "I'm worried about her. She's not been sleeping properly. She's been having hallucinations. She thought she saw someone in her room the first night we were here."

Mark must react in some way because Mum's voice changes. She sounds annoyed. "It's not that surprising, is it? Out here!" She's standing at the window, her face pressed against the glass. I can see it clouding over.

"There'll be another boat in a couple of days," Mark

says, resting his hand on her shoulder. "More equipment coming in."

"Another boat?" Mum says, brushing him off and sounding upset now. "Why on earth are they sending more equipment? We haven't been given the final sign-off."

Mark laughs. "It will come." He rubs his fingers together triumphantly like he's counting out banknotes. "Andrei will make sure it comes."

I can't see the expression on Mum's face but she puts her right hand up to her forehead. Her voice is tired. "I wish I could think more clearly. I'm getting such bad headaches. I'm not sure this place is good for me."

Mark tuts impatiently. "You're distracted. It's understandable, with your daughter to worry about. You should send her back on the boat to Longyearbyen. Ingrid could organize the flight for her. Your husband could meet her."

"He's not my husband," Mum says automatically, but she doesn't refute his suggestion about sending me away.

I slink back to my room and collapse on my bed. How can Mum talk about me behind my back, with Mark of all people?

I don't get up when Mum comes in. I stay turned to the wall, staring at the whale pictures. They're so familiar now.

There's a false brightness in Mum's voice. "How was the glacier, kiddo?"

I don't answer. Kiddo? When did she ever call me that? It's one of Dad's names for me.

"Rory?" Mum says, moving closer and shutting the door behind her. "Did something happen? Are you OK?"

"We saw another reindeer," I say, rolling over to face her. "A dead one."

Mum crouches by my bed to stroke my hair. "I'm sorry, Rory. How sad."

I push her hand away. Sad?! It's more than sad. "Why aren't Greenlight doing anything? Why aren't they investigating?" I cry.

"They have," Mum says. "I told you. It's not related, my love. The townspeople want to sabotage the Rare Earths Project."

"Why aren't we listening to them? They know better than Andrei and Mark, Mum!" My eyebrows knot together. "You do know who was here first, don't you? You do remember that? This is their home."

"Yes," Mum says in a lecturing tone. "And yet Andrei will have them moved on if they get in the way. He's already threatening to, and he's not known for his patience."

"Then the townspeople will be even more hostile! They already hate you all!"

Mum gets up and wanders to the window restlessly. I stay on my bed, staring up at the ceiling, angry tears brimming in my eyes.

"I wonder if it's a good idea for you to spend quite so much time with them," Mum says after a couple of minutes. "The other children, I mean. Have you done anything for school since you got here?" She indicates the pile of books in the corner, the maths set on top shining in its tin case. "I worry the children here are a bad influence on you."

I stare at her in disbelief. "You're always on at me to make friends and when I finally do, you want me to sit in my room alone and do some work?"

"All this!" Mum gestures with her hand to the cold world outside. "This isn't your real world, Rory! We'll be going home soon, leaving it all behind. How you do at school matters for the rest of your life. The children here wouldn't understand, it's not their fault, but they're uneducated."

I yelp in frustration. "You don't know half the things they know. About reindeer, and the ice and the whales and the way everything fits together. You could learn from them. Greenlight *should* be learning from them."

Mum sighs. "I'm not denying it, Rory. Honestly, I admire them. How they've even managed to stay alive out here, winter after winter. I'm not sure I could! Yet Greenlight has some of the best scientists and engineers in the Northern Hemisphere and you don't know the lengths they're going to in order to accommodate these people. Who shouldn't even be here, I might add."

"Where else would they be?" I snap.

Faint patches of red have crept on to Mum's cheeks. She slumps down on the desk chair. "Mark says they're being offered housing south of the Arctic Circle. In Norway, Sweden, Finland, Russia. Greenlight would organize transport, there are housing projects that would still accept them."

"Accept them?" I say, horrified that these words are spilling out of Mum's mouth. "After everything the people here have been through. They love this place. What if they want to stay and help look after it?"

"It might be best for them. Safer. The children here should be growing up with the advantages you have! Those older kids, Mikkal, Ivan's daughter Nina – you don't think they deserve to study science and maths and music? You don't think they deserve those opportunities?"

I screw my face up. Is Mum right? Would Mikkal and Nina and the others jump at the chance to go to school? What about Mikkal going to live in a forest with the reindeer, like his mum's people used to?

"It's not everything. Your kind of education. Your kind of opportunities," I say sullenly, though there's a waver in my voice now.

Mum sits back down on the bed and gathers me up into an embrace. "I know you haven't been happy lately. I know that, Rory."

I stay rigid in her arms.

"You're such a brilliant girl. We will make it better for you when we get back. I promise. You'll make friends again." Mum strokes my hair and clasps her palms around my cheeks.

"I'm making friends *here*," I cry, shaking a little now. "You don't see it because you're always working."

"We've got a date for the Arctic Council coming now." Mum's face collapses a little as she says it. Those lines on the sides of her eyes, deep, like tracks in the snow. "It's in just a few days' time. I'm going to be head down doing my report till then, but after that I'm hoping I'll be done here. We can arrange transport home."

"Home?" I say in astonishment. Home seems so far away. And Dad's forest. Dad most of all. I feel a pulse of anger at him being so disconnected there and his last question from our phone call nags at me. What do I think about the reindeer? If the Arctic Council are visiting so soon, we're running out of time to tell the truth.

Mum's nodding gently. "Home." She gives me a squeeze. "But I'd better get on. My report won't finish itself. No rest for the wicked."

"Mum," I call as she gets to the door. There's no changing her mind. She's fully in Greenlight's grip. I know now what I have to do. "Do you have a spare key for that new room? Maybe I could work there, with you? I find it hard being in my room sometimes. Alone.

The noises, you know?"

Mum smiles with relief. "Of course. I could do with some company. Pia wasn't wrong about this place feeling lonely, and you're right, we've barely seen each other lately, have we?"

"So you have a key you can give me?"

Mum shakes her head casually. "I'll just leave it unlocked for you. I'm sure it's fine. No one comes up here, do they? You can go in whenever you like."

I smile back guiltily, but I'm pleased too, that I've paved my way to access the maps. "Thanks, Mum."

# Footsteps

Over on the other side of town, the dogs are barking in their kennels.

I lie awake, my brain whirring. The dead eyes of the reindeer by the whaling station won't leave my mind. Or the belugas swimming in the bay.

What happens when a bear comes to take the reindeer carcass? Or when it gets washed into the sea? Any dangerous chemicals won't end with the reindeer. And what about the people who rely on their meat to stay alive?

I stand up to turn on the light and catch sight of my face in the mirror, my hair wild and thick with salt from the boat trip. I look like I belong here now.

Another face appears beside mine, like a shadow or reflection of my own. A pale white face, but with light hair, blond, where mine is amber red. Brown eyes, piercing into mine. Not with meanness, with something else.

I turn around to catch them.

There's no one, and I cry out in frustration. "Who are you? What do you want?"

I open my door to look down the blank space of the corridor either side. There's only the cavity of the staircase.

I stop to listen. There are clear footsteps above me. Definitely not birds, as they've all left before the deepest part of winter. Except the ptarmigans on the slopes outside town, tough, loyal, white save for their black eyes.

There's the voice now, half singing. *Rory. Rory.*

I make myself follow the steps upwards again, back through the ceiling to the floor above. Stepping over the feathers and droppings and all the leftover things. It's not my business to be up here, trespassing through old lives.

*Rory. Rory.*

The voice is in my head, I tell myself, unsure if this should be a relief, when something catches my eye. Over by the window. Light, reflection.

Yet not light. It's more a disturbance of the air. A flutter of something.

I creep further through the stacks of old things. It's all junk.

The light that's not really light settles on a stack of photos. They're faded – in summertime, the sun must shine through to them, bleaching the old inks.

I flick through them, a tingling sensation at the back of my head as I recognize Pyramiden. Paris, London, the Cultural Palace. The swimming pool, with shining water. The polar bear mosaic. The grey-black mountain with the gallery leading up its incline. The mine looks operational in the photos. There are men with blackened faces, smiling into the sun. Sadness fills my chest, because I know some of these people will have died when the mine collapsed.

There's a photo of a hut with smoke circling out of its chimney and a reindeer skin hanging on a hook outside. There's a kitchen table, back in the town, with a carved carcass being cut into different sections, no part of the animal wasted. There's even a woman stirring a bucketful of blood and another of a pan of soup with antlers sticking out of the top ceremonially.

And living reindeer too – and people among them. A child taking a ride on one, peering inquisitively at the camera. A woman feeding a bottle of milk to a young calf.

The animals mean so much to the people here.

"Are you here, in the photos?" I whisper, skimming them for the face in the mirror. Is this why they led me up here? Did they want to show me how important the reindeer are for this place? But the voice has gone quiet now, and after a while I go back down to my cold room, to dream of whales and polar bears. A bowhead, two centuries old, breaking through the ice for seals. A mother bear, playing on the tundra with her cubs, blood on their mouths as they tear apart a reindeer corpse.

# Betrayal

I make my way to Mum's new office room before breakfast, feeling a fresh sense of purpose after last night's trip to the floor above. Mum must already be having breakfast, or gone off somewhere.

There's the annotated map in full sight on her desk. It looks like Mum's been using it every day. Why can't she see it for what it is and make the connection with the reindeer? This thought pushes away the twisting guilt that crawls around my gut as I snap photos of the different sections of the map, and the different plans and diagrams beneath it. Anything that shows locations around Pyramiden.

I bump into Ingrid on the way out.

"Rory?" she addresses me suspiciously. "Whatever were you doing in there?"

"It's my mum's office," I stumble. "She said I could.

I'm working there too now."

"Really?" Ingrid looks surprised. "I hope Andrei doesn't hear about that. You mustn't distract her."

"Of course not," I say, pushing past her.

Back outside in the square, white flakes drift to the hard ground. I catch them in my gloved fingers as I make my way to the Cultural Palace to look for Mikkal.

I still haven't seen thick snow. Just the light scatterings the townspeople clear from the walkways every day, to keep them free of ice. This snow floats down like feathers. I hold my face up, to taste it on my tongue, and it falls on to my eyelids. Delicious soft crystals of it. It doesn't feel wet, or sting like the snow that comes in with the wind, falling in blades. This is the snow I'd longed for.

I press on, to scan the lower floor of the Cultural Palace, but Mikkal is nowhere to be seen and the building rings with emptiness.

I'm about to leave when I hear raised voices in one of the upstairs rooms. I glance up just as Jonne stumbles down past me. I jump into the doorway opposite.

I don't think he even sees me. The door swings shut behind him, the slam echoing through the silent rooms. I begin to make my own way out when I hear crying from upstairs. I know at once it's Pia.

I tiptoe up the stairs and creak open the door. Pia gives a fleeting look of disappointment when she sees it's me.

She's sat by the window.

"Did you hear that?" she asks, wiping her eyes as I enter the room.

"No," I say quickly. Too quickly. My cheeks burn red. Then, "I wasn't eavesdropping. I was looking for Mikkal."

Pia smiles kindly. "I love seeing the kids tear through this place. I'm glad you're getting to know them, Rory. I knew you'd fit in."

I smile back and take one of the metal chairs by the wall. It squeaks against the floor.

"I think Jonne wishes he was still that age, running off to watch whales with his best friend," Pia says, looking out now at the falling snow. There's an edge of bitterness in her voice.

A cold draught blows through the building. I can hear the door below still banging after Jonne's dramatic departure. He can't have shut it properly.

Pia wraps her arms round herself and shivers. "Listen to me! I've been drinking too much coffee. Not getting enough sleep." She sighs wistfully. "It was different here in the summer. There was sun like you wouldn't believe."

I smile, trying to work out what response to give.

Pia pulls at the skin on her face. "This icy wind is getting to me. Soon I'll be as weathered as those old mountains."

Our eyes travel together to the mountain above us. The rolling scree, covered in snow, ridged and hard. I read that frost attacks the mountains here from both directions.

The snow is falling much thicker and faster now.

I'm about to tell Pia about the pictures of the map on my phone, that I've done what they asked me to, when she grasps my hand. "Don't listen to Jonne, Rory. It'll only get your mum into trouble. We had to sign all kinds of secrecy clauses to work here. Andrei's already on the war path. It wasn't fair, what Jonne asked you to do. What *we* asked you to do," Pia says, looking at me worriedly. "I promise I didn't know Jonne was going to do that. I really did just want to show you the glacier."

I stay silent, my phone cold in my pocket. Could the photos really get my mum into trouble?

Pia breathes out slowly. "I'm cross with him. As you can see!"

"Is that what you were arguing about?" I ask, puzzled. Surely it's right that I would help Jonne try to save the reindeer?

"No, no," Pia says quickly. "Most of the time I don't even know what we argue about. Jonne thinks this place will be signed away and changed forever. Broken. He thinks I should be doing more to stop it, but he doesn't know what it's like in that office. Everyone's so paranoid now." There's a slight hiss in her voice.

"Do you think my mum knows Greenlight has made mistakes?" I press, keen to see what Pia will say about Mum away from Jonne.

Pia shrugs. "Honestly, I don't know any more. But I do know it's good your mum is here. We needed someone like her." She swallows and wipes away a tear.

I nod slowly, thinking of Mum stepping off the plane, new and excited, and how she is now. Her thin shoulders, tight together, like branches grown warped in the wind. What has this place done to her? To us?

"Could there be another child here I haven't met yet?" I ask Pia suddenly. "A girl, about my age, with blond hair?"

Pia puts her head to the side. "Nina, maybe? Her hair is light."

"Not Nina. Someone else!" I grip the sides of the metal chair.

Pia looks mystified. "I'm sure you've met everyone there is to meet. I can't think of anyone else."

I nod reluctantly. "Yes, of course," I say, getting up to go.

"Are you OK, Rory? I'm sure everything will get sorted. You can leave it to the adults," Pia says. She rubs at her red eyes and laughs. "Most of them are more together than me!"

I smile, though I've already made my decision. I made it yesterday on the beach by the old whaling station, and it was confirmed last night on the top floor of Paris. Mum won't want to sign off on a project that condemns Svalbard's inhabitants to more destruction. Whether Pia wants to be part of it or not, I'm going to make sure Jonne gets the photos.

211

# Snow

I force open the door leading to the square. The children are gathering snow and rolling it into balls.

Shouts and laughter float through the still air. Everything's muffled in the new softness of the landscape and I freeze for a moment staring at the moving forms, trying to work out who everyone is.

"Rory!" Mikkal shouts, spotting me in the doorway. I hesitate, wondering what the others will make of me joining in, but then a snowball hits my chest and I can't resist any longer. Haven't I been hoping for snow like this all my life?

I step outside, my boots crunching, and bend down for a fresh handful to hurl back in the direction I was hit from. A boy shrieks with laughter and stoops to retaliate. Kaiku's bouncing around excitedly, burying her face into the snow, to emerge a few seconds later, her blue nose covered in crystals and her mouth hanging in a wide grin.

"Rory! Rory!" a couple of the smaller ones chime. Nina glances over in my direction. She smiles before she takes aim, and I sidestep to avoid the missile.

"Next time!" she calls, giggling.

Today I'm one of them. We play girls against boys, and me, Nina, Buppha, Nan, Hilda and a couple of the littles work together to force the boys off the walkway they've claimed and round the corner of the Cultural Palace.

"We claim victory!" they chant, and I join in at full pitch. Clearly the battle to control the walkways is an established format for the game.

At some point the snowballs stop flying as intensely, and I join Mikkal crafting a snowy form on four legs, with a pointed face and distinctive bushy tail. "It's a friend for you, Kaiku!" We laugh, as the two foxes meet nose to nose. One sculpted in white, one blue and rippling with life. Around us, others build snow people, with hard stones for eyes, mouths and teeth.

There's a collective sudden realization of how cold we are, and cheeks red, fingers burning, we flock into the canteen for hot drinks.

Some Greenlight employees at a table by the door mutter loud disapproval as we come in. I hear them talking about me. "Laura's daughter." I glare disdainfully, turning my back on them, proud to be with the town's children. Mum and I have been here almost four weeks now and most of the Greenlight people still don't know my name.

After our hot chocolates, some of the kids begin a game of tag, and bump into one of the Greenlight tables. A pot of coffee spills across the wood.

"For goodness' sake!" Mark shouts, leaping to his feet, flapping papers. "This is not a nursery!"

The kids shriek with laughter and run out into the square. I start after them but Mark puts out his foot to stop me, and grabs hold of my arm.

"What are you doing?" I cry, struggling to get free.

"What are you doing with them? We expect better of you. You do understand how badly this reflects on your mother!" His voice quivers threateningly, and my heart thuds against my chest.

"We're at a crucial stage of the project," he goes on. "We don't need these distractions. Do you want to mess things up for her?" His grip on my arm tightens.

Mikkal has doubled back into the cafeteria. "What's happening?" he asks, his eyes darting between us. "Rory, are you OK?"

Mark loosens his hold, and I take the chance to wrench my arm free. I stagger backwards.

"I'm reminding this young lady who she is," Mark hisses. "And under whose terms she was permitted to come here!

Running around with you and the rest of your reprobates."

A flicker of confusion crosses Mikkal's face. "We're not reprobates!" He stumbles over the word.

Mark sneers at his mispronunciation.

"This is our home!" Mikkal retaliates, puffing up his chest now, like the ptarmigans out on the slopes. "Why shouldn't we run around? It's you that's destroying it."

Mark's sneer only increases.

I try to pull Mikkal away, tears in my eyes, feeling strange and sick at Mark's behaviour. "He's not worth it. Leave it."

"No!" Mikkal cries indignantly. "Why do we have to make things so easy for them! We were here first, Rory!" He stamps his foot on the floor. "This is our home!"

"Illegally," Mark says harshly. "We'll see what the Arctic Council say about your 'settlement' when they make their assessment."

"What do you mean?" Mikkal answers, furious now. "Just you wait. We'll prove what you're doing…"

"Mikkal!" I plead. "Leave it!"

Mark continues to goad him as I drag Mikkal out to the square to calm down. By the side of the Cultural Palace, where the air vents whirr, a reindeer is collapsed on the snow. We both run towards it.

Mikkal crouches beside the creature and coos gently at her in Norwegian. I've learned enough to know this one is a girl. She's panting heavily. Snow has gathered around her, collecting over her velvety antlers. She must have been here all the time we were out playing.

"I could get Rasmos," I offer.

Mikkal shakes his head, looking up at me, pulling his hair out of his eyes. "It's not worth it. It's kinder to leave her. They can take her away when she's gone."

When she's dead, I know he means.

"Have you decided, about what Jonne asked you?" Mikkal says, his face hard-edged and his voice bitter. "I can't stand having those people here. Looking down on us. How can they not see what they're doing? *You* see, don't you? You see what it's like?"

I hand Mikkal my phone silently. He stays crouched beside the reindeer and takes his hand out of his glove, blowing on his fingers to warm then. Then he scrolls through the photos of the maps.

"Did anyone see you take these?" he asks quietly.

I shake my head, shivering, and brush snow away from the reindeer's face.

"Ingrid was there, but I don't think she suspected anything."

The reindeer's breath is warm on my fingers.

"Can I borrow this?" Mikkal asks, holding up my phone. "To show Jonne?"

"Of course," I say, a little fire set alight in my chest, imagining what Mark and Andrei would think if they knew what I was doing. Laura's daughter.

"Mikkal?" I say, as he makes to get up. My turn to ask a favour.

He tilts his head to listen.

"Will you come to the top floor of Building Nine with me?"

"Paris?" he says, surprised. Clearly it's not what he was expecting. "There's nothing up there, is there? Just a load of junk."

My voice is stilted but certain. "I found some photos, from before the mine collapsed. I want you to look through them with me."

"Why, Rory?" His eyes dig into me. I keep my eyes on the reindeer, stroking her rhythmically, watching her breathing slow.

"It's something to do with that girl I thought I saw. And the noises I've been hearing. I hear them every night now." I swallow.

"You think you'll see the girl in the old photos, Rory? You don't believe what Nina said about ghosts?"

"Of course not," I say, shrugging off his stare. "I just want to know more about who used to live here."

"Sure, then," Mikkal breathes, getting up with my phone in hand. "I'll come and find you as soon as I've given this to Jonne."

# Faces

"Eww, Rory," Mikkal says as we reach the top floor of Building Nine, sighting the bird dirt and clumps of plaster where the walls are slowly disintegrating. He screws up his face. "This is a bird toilet. No wonder no one comes up here."

"At the end," I say, urging him on. "Over by the window. Please, Mikkal. I'll go first."

He rolls his eyes but follows me through the discarded things. The floorboards creak under our feet.

Mikkal lets out a low whistle when he spies the old books and papers against the windows.

We kneel down, blowing away a layer of grey dust from the stacks of photos.

I push a pile across to him. "I need to know if you recognize any of these people."

Mikkal glances at me warily. I don't want to drag him back to Pyramiden's tragic history, but I need to know who she is. The voice. The footsteps. The face in the mirror. There must be a reason she appears to me.

The top photos are of a group of people, seated in front of the polar bear mosaic in the auditorium. Four rows of children. A few of the older ones have infants on their laps.

"Jonne," Mikkal whispers, pointing to one of the children. He's standing in the back row. You can only see half his face because it's turned to the side, to look at a girl with long blond hair loose around her shoulders.

"That's Ulya," Mikkal breathes. "Jonne's got pictures he drew of her in his room. I bet he doesn't know about these photos."

"Jonne draws?" I ask.

Mikkal shakes his head. "Used to. Now he just carves his animals."

"How can you be sure it's Ulya?" I ask, looking back to the photo. You can't see the girl's face properly. Just the edge of her smile as she turns to face Jonne.

"I swear it's her. It makes sense, the way they're looking at each other. Mum always says they were inseparable," Mikkal goes on, whispering, as if the people in the photo are listening.

"Ulya," I whisper back. She doesn't want to be lined up for a staged photo, she wants to be running off to play hide-and-seek or flying high into the sky on the swings in the square. Or taking the dogs out for a run with the sleds. I know this. I know it all as clearly as if I were feeling it myself.

Mikkal turns the picture over and reads the date on the back. Twelve years ago.

"That's just a few days before the mine collapsed," he says sombrely. "This must be one of the last photos of everyone together. Ulya was the youngest to die in the accident."

"What about her parents? Are they still here in the town?"

"Mum says they went back to Ukraine after the accident. They can't have seen any reason to stay. We should have gone too."

He blinks quickly and screws up his face, as though he's imagining a different life. Maybe a school, a classroom somewhere, with more kids his age. With science labs and music rooms and sports fields, just like mine. Can you imagine a place like that if you've never seen it? Maybe he's imagining a forest and travelling with the reindeer like his mum's people used to do.

"What made you come up here?" Mikkal asks suddenly, looking at me afresh.

"I don't know. I felt…" I start.

"What did you feel, Rory?" Mikkal presses, leaning in closer. Our breath is fogging up the window.

"Mikkal! Mikkal!" It's his mum somewhere below calling him.

Mikkal peers guiltily through the smeared glass. "She sounds worried. She must know I'm not with the others."

"Go," I insist. There's no way I'm leaving the photos now. Not without my answer.

"Are you sure, Rory?" Mikkal says, walking to the stairs reluctantly. "I don't like to leave you here."

"I'm fine, I promise," I say, forcing a smile and urging him again to go.

I carry on flicking through the rest of the photo stack. Mikkal steps back for a moment from the top of the steps, like he's scared I'll be dragged into the photos and frozen in time. But then his mum calls again, more frantically now, and he disappears into the main part of the building, his footsteps clattering all the way down.

Towards the bottom of the box are individual portraits. Each person is stood in the exact same spot, on the bottom of the staircase of the Cultural Palace as it starts to turn upwards in its distinctive spiral. My frayed sofa would have been out of sight behind the steps.

Some of the people in the photos are smiling. Some are more formal or even moody, like when I had to get the photo taken for my passport and was told I couldn't smile.

I almost drop the next photo I come to, and my torch falls to the floor and rolls around in the bird dirt and feathers. I pick it up to illuminate the face.

My hand trembles. She's staring right at the camera and her name's written underneath in tiny handwriting, in the exact same script of the whale pictures. Ulya.

Forever fourteen years old. The face I saw in the mirror.

# Departure

I blunder into the snowy square, past the formless figures of the snow people. I'm not sure where I'm headed. Mikkal will be safely indoors with his mum. The other children too, with heaters on full blast. I'm just not ready to go back to my room yet.

Why is Jonne's friend haunting me?

"Rory!" a voice calls from behind me.

"Pia," I say, turning with relief. I want to throw myself into her arms. She steps towards me and I notice the rucksack on her back.

"Where are you going?" My voice tremors.

"Rory," Pia begins. Her eyes are red and tears glisten on her cheeks.

"You're leaving?" I ask, unable to believe what I'm seeing.

"I never planned to stay the whole winter. I told you that."

"So you're just leaving? Before the Arctic Council visit?" I cry, tears pricking at my eyes. "You're abandoning my mum?"

"That's not fair," Pia says, flinching. "I'm not abandoning anyone. I was brought over to survey the glacier and it turns out Andrei doesn't even want me to do that properly. All he wants is written proof that the mine won't damage the glacier further."

"And will it?" I ask, thinking about standing on the blue ice and how you could hear it talking. The way Pia bent close to listen, as if she could hear its heartbeat. It's the same as when Mikkal talks to the reindeer.

Pia throws her arms out in despair. "It might, Rory. It might! All of this, and your world too, back in England, and mine in Sweden – it's connected, isn't it? There's always a price to pay for every bit of progress. Like Jonne said in that meeting. Not that they listened." Pia gives a cry of rage. "They never listen!"

I grit my teeth, knowing she's right. Andrei will make the reports say whatever they need to, to get Greenlight their licence. I gulp. "My mum won't give up on the project now. It could damage her reputation."

Pia nods. "I understand that. I understand why she thinks she should stay. But listen, Rory, the boat's in the harbour. The *Leviathan*. You could come with me. The captain would wait for you, I know he would."

There's a faint yellow from over near the harbour, like light from another world.

I look back to the windows of Building Nine, in case Mum is looking out for me, worried I'm lost in the snow. Would she drag me back inside? Or perhaps she'd insist I pack my bags and go with Pia. Truth is, I don't know how Mum will react any more. She's changed here, just like I have.

I shake my head. "I can't leave my mum."

"She'd understand," Pia goes on. "Your mum must see by now that this place isn't meant for people like us. I could deliver you back to Tromsø."

I picture the bright lights of the airport, with its round window overlooking the town. Picture book perfect. That would have been adventure enough. The trip of a lifetime. We shouldn't have come so far north. Greenlight shouldn't be here either, hacking open the mountains all over again. Is that why Ulya has been coming to my room at night? Is she warning me away or asking for my help?

If I went back to Tromsø, it's one more plane back to England, and Dad's cabin in the woods. There would still be trails of colour there – reds, yellows, golds. But how would me leaving help Mum? And the reindeer?

I just found out who she is. Ulya. Ulya who loved the whales. Jonne's friend. It's impossible to tell all this to Pia, out here, on the icy wood. She's clearly already made up her mind to leave.

"You're shivering! You must get back inside," Pia urges, though for a moment she comes closer, and pulls me into a hug with her mittened fingers. "It was nice to get to meet you, Rory."

I start to cry properly now. Warm tears on my freezing cold cheeks.

"Say goodbye to your mum for me," Pia says, her voice breaking a little. "You should hear her – the way she stands up to Andrei. You'd be proud of her."

A horn sounds from the waterside and Pia lets go of me, beads of frost on her eyelashes.

"Go, Rory, inside. Get warm."

I watch her stepping along the wooden walkway. I know I won't see her again. She'll disappear into her own life, and these weeks in Svalbard will be lost in time.

"Don't forget me!" she calls, before hurrying along the path for her passage home.

# Sabotage

Mum charges into my room just as I've changed for bed. She slams the door shut behind her. "I need to talk to you, Rory," she says, her voice jittery.

"What?" I ask, unease prickling over my skin. Has Jonne done something with the maps I photographed already?

"Did you go into my office today?"

"No!"

"While I was having dinner?" Mum takes hold of my shoulders and shakes me a little.

"Mum!" I shout. "No! You're scaring me!" My heart starts to beat faster. Ingrid must have seen me photographing the maps.

"Mum looks back to the door. "Can I trust you, Rory?"

"Of course you can trust me!" I say instantly, though I feel sick inside.

Mum nods her head slowly. "My report's gone. Gone in its entirety," Mum says.

"Gone?" I repeat, unsure what she means.

"Gone. Deleted without trace. Like it was never there, Rory!" Mum's eyes are wide.

"But I didn't, I would never…" I stumble. "I mean, I know how hard you've been working on it, Mum!"

"I need you to tell me the truth, Rory. I know how worried you are about the reindeer, and everything the townspeople have been telling you about the mine."

"I would never delete your report, Mum," I cut in insistently.

Mum's face opens in relief. She kisses the top of my head. "I'm sorry, Rory. Of course you wouldn't. I'm just tired. Forgive me." She takes a deep breath and wraps her arms round me. "Poor you, in your freezing cold room. The last thing you need is accusations from me. I shouldn't have listened to Mark. I should have trusted myself. I knew straight away it was Jonne."

"Jonne?" I voice, pulling away from her. "Jonne wouldn't do that."

"He doesn't want us to be here," Mum goes on intently. "He couldn't have been any clearer at that meeting. Dragging up the entire history of this island like Greenlight should be blamed for all of it."

"He was just trying to make a point about how precious

things are here, and how fragile," I clutch. "This place is amazing, Mum. If you'd seen the whales in the bay, and if you'd met the reindeer… It isn't the place for mining any more. Maybe it never was."

Mum stares at me sadly. "Don't you trust me, Rory? Don't you see how hard I'm working to give the full picture, so the Arctic Council has all the information to make the right decision? My report's important for that, and now it's disappeared into thin air."

"Jonne wouldn't have deleted it," I say again, knowing I'm right. That's not how he'd work.

"It's deleted from the back-up too," Mum's saying. "Whoever did it did a thorough job. They knew what they were doing."

"Can't you rewrite it?" I ask.

Mum splutters. "Do you realize how many hours, days, weeks of work have gone into it, Rory?"

"I just thought, with your notes—"

"Oh, Rory!" Mum says, cutting me off. "I wish it were that easy. So much of the associated data has gone too. I'm going to have to go back through all my notebooks and see what I can still make sense of. I don't even have Pia around to help."

"I'm sorry, Mum."

She moves closer to me and her fingers tease the knots in my hair. It's tangled from the Arctic wind. She places her palms around my cheeks and examines my face. "You have shadows under your eyes."

"It's just lack of sunlight. You have them too," I say, rolling my eyes. Neither of us is doing that well, going by appearances.

"We'll be back home soon, I promise," Mum says, as if to comfort me.

My toes curl in my slippers. I don't want to think about going back. "What if this place is good for me?" I whisper. "What if this place is where I can be myself?"

Mum looks at me strangely. "Listen, Rory, don't worry about the report. It'll all be fine in the end. I'm sorry we're not getting the time we wanted to hang out."

"It doesn't matter now," I say, my mouth in a thin smile. "I really am happy here. You do what you need to do."

# Expedition

Mikkal calls me over the instant I enter the canteen for breakfast. He's sitting up straight, an excited look on his face.

"I was waiting for you! Jonne's taking the dogs out, with Nina's dad. On a proper run. We're going to stay overnight in a couple of huts north of here." He gives me a meaningful look. "You should come with us!"

"Me?" I exclaim, glancing sideways at the others.

"You have to experience the dog sleds while you're here. There's nothing like it!" He passes my phone across the table pointedly. Nina eyes it suspiciously. "Rory let me borrow it overnight," Mikkal says by way of explanation. "I was showing Mum her forest pictures. You know how she misses trees. Jonne was interested too." He winks at me.

"Jonne just wants a distraction from Pia going," Nina

231

grumbles. "I heard she didn't even say goodbye."

Mikkal purposefully ignores her. "You have to come on the sleds, Rory. You can get a proper look at this place."

"Do you think Jonne would let me?" I ask, trembling at the thought of travelling with the dogs and seeing if we can finally find out what's going on here. What Greenlight has been hiding.

And leaving the town. Going even further north, before I go back to England forever.

"I'll persuade him," Mikkal says with new swagger. "But we have to go now. They're getting ready."

"Why do you want to come with us?" Jonne asks when we find him by the dog huts. The dogs have got wind of the trip – a ripple of anticipation runs through them, their tails high in the air.

"I want to see for myself," I start, gulping, not wanting to mess this up. Jonne's angular face has extra shadows on it today, and I feel a new wave of sadness at Pia's departure. It's not just me and Mum she's abandoned.

"If my mum hasn't got time to see this place properly, maybe it's up to me to go in her place," I go on.

Jonne's still busy with the dogs, pulling individual ones out to strap on harnesses. The chosen ones for the trip!

"And Rory did get us the map," Mikkal reminds him. "We owe her."

"No," Jonne says sternly now, glaring at his brother. "We don't owe anyone anything." He turns to me gravely. "Rory, you understand I can't take responsibility for your safety out there?"

"Of course," I breathe.

"And your mum understands that too?"

I nod quickly. Although I haven't even thought about how I'll persuade Mum.

"OK then," Jonne says curtly, over his shoulder now, already walking away. "Find out from Ivan what to pack." He indicates over to one of the huts, where Ivan's uncovering a wooden sled. "We leave in an hour."

"Why did Pia leave, do you think?" I ask, as we head over to Ivan.

"Jonne won't talk about her," Mikkal says. "I think he drove her away. He needs to learn to be friendlier. That's what Mum says too."

I turn for a second to watch Jonne striding back to the main buildings. He looks like he has the weight of the world on his shoulders. I still don't reckon Jonne would have deleted Mum's report, but whoever did has bought us more time to investigate. Could deleting it have been Pia's parting gift? She's so obviously in love with him.

It makes me uncomfortable to think about, that Pia

would betray Mum, even if she was doing it to save this place. But I push this feeling away. Right now I have to persuade Mum to let me go on a trip into the true winter wilderness.

# Persuasion

"Absolutely not! You're not leaving the settlement without me!"

"Can't you even listen to the plans?" I answer back, frustrated. "It's only going to be for a couple of nights. Jonne is taking us, and Ivan."

"Jonne?" Mum exclaims. "Is that meant to be reassuring for me? That meeting was when things started to turn sour here."

"He was their spokesperson that day, Mum! Isn't it good to question things? Isn't that what you're doing too, by being here? Pia told me how you stand up to Andrei. She said I would be proud of you!"

Mum softens a little at these last words, but she shakes her head. "Regardless of who is leading this expedition, it's a safety issue. The dark, the ice, the bears, the desolation.

Need I go on?"

"They're used to these things! They've lived here their whole lives."

"Yes, but *you* haven't, Rory. You've grown up in suburbia."

"Not just suburbia. I live part time in the forest now." I don't like how Mum ignores this bit of my life, even though it's part of me.

"It's hardly the same thing!" Mum says. "A woodland in England doesn't prepare you for an Arctic wilderness!"

"I want to get away from this building for a while," I say, changing tactic, desperate to get her to agree. "When I was anxious about school, you told me to go for a run, or a swim, to use up some nervous energy. What if I need to use up some energy now too? You know how badly I've been sleeping."

"What about the sports hall…?" Mum offers.

"The sports hall isn't even heated and there's no water in the pool. Mum! You know all this! You've been out on the skidoo while I've been cooped up here. It's not fair! I deserve an adventure too."

Mum's face doesn't waver.

"Like you promised me," I slip in.

She fixes her eyes on mine. "And Jonne is happy to take responsibility for you?"

"Absolutely," I say, with just a touch of guilt. I don't want to get Jonne into trouble just because I want to go dog sledding. But it's more than that. It feels as if I'm meant to go. If I can help prove what's going on with the reindeer, I can help Mum have the right information, the truth, to present to the Arctic Council. I know if she had space and light in her head to see the full picture, it'd make sense to her.

I can see her resolve slipping. "Well, I am going to be ridiculously busy over the next couple of days, especially with the lost report, and Pia leaving out of the blue. I still can't believe she did that."

She gazes out of the window of her office towards the old mine. I wonder if she has the same thoughts about who might have deleted her report.

"So what about me going? On the dog sled?" I prompt.

"Maybe I should clear it with your dad," she murmurs. "If we can get the satellite phone working again, or send an email."

"There isn't time! Jonne and Ivan are getting ready to set off soon so we maximize the light. Mum!" I cry. Across town I can hear the dogs barking. What if they go without me?

Mum lets out a deep breath. "OK, Rory. But you have to promise to stay within sight of them at all times and obey every single instruction. I'd never forgive myself if anything happened to you."

"It won't," I say, hugging her with gratitude.

She smiles at me almost with relief, and even though a moment ago I was desperate for her to say yes, I feel weirdly abandoned by it.

# Musher

Mikkal and I hurry to the dog sleds together. Kaiku is trotting at our feet, ears pricked up, tail in the air. She can sense this is no ordinary trip.

"Isn't your mum coming to see you off?" Mikkal asks.

"I don't think so," I say, taking a lingering glance back towards our building. It's only just starting to get light. "She was going back to the mine. To repeat some measurements she'd lost. The delegation from the Arctic Council arrives in a few days."

"Will she include it in her report if we find anything?" Mikkal asks. He didn't hide his joy when I told him about Mum having to start it again.

I nod my head affirmatively. "If we had actual evidence…" I pat my yellow camera, which I've stuffed safely under my coat and two layers of jumpers. I've got my phone too, fully charged and turned off in my bag. Ivan instructed us to pack light and bring only essentials for keeping warm and fed, but how else are we going to get everyone to believe us? Pictures are meant to say a thousand words.

"Mikkal! Rory! Come on!" Jonne shouts impatiently, spying us from inside the kennels. "We want to be going!"

Rasmos opens the gate for us, the posts scraping over the snow. "You're dressed warmly enough? The temperature plummets the moment you get outside the settlement," he addresses me, his eyes darting between the mountains in the distance and the white snowfields between.

"I'm ready," I say, sounding braver than I feel, nervous they'll change their minds about taking me.

The dogs surge forwards to surround us, their tongues hanging out in excitement. Their yelps get louder, and little bells sound from round their necks.

"So we don't lose them," Rasmos explains. "The snow will be much deeper outside of town, and away from the coast."

"Don't they get cold?" I ask, bending down to stroke them. Their fur moves in ripples in the wind.

"These dogs were bred for the cold," Rasmos says. "They like it better the colder it is! We're heading into their favourite season."

One of the dogs pushes its warm nose into me.

"That's Ajax," Rasmos says, as the dog rolls over at my feet showing a white and silky belly. "He's only a couple of years old. He's going to be leading one of the sleds. Are you going to be musher, Rory? He looks like he's chosen you."

"Musher?" I ask, stroking the dog's tummy energetically and contemplating his distinctive eyes, one icy blue, one amber. I've never seen an animal with different coloured eyes before. "Hello, Ajax," I coo at him.

"The musher is the driver!" Ivan explains, beside us suddenly and tapping me on the shoulder in welcome. "You should try it, Rory. There's nothing like it."

"Oh no, I don't think so," I say, stepping back uncertainly and almost stumbling over another of the dogs. "I've never... I've never done anything like that before."

"You've got to have a go," Mikkal insists, shoving me gently forwards. "You're not still frightened of them, are you?"

"Not of the dogs!" I scoff, though there is something about the frothing, yipping mound of dogs that unnerves me. They'd be off in a heartbeat if they were let go.

"You two will ride together," Jonne announces brusquely, coming alongside and making the decision for us. "Mikkal will drive. You'll ride in the basket, Rory. You'll be safe. Mikkal's one of the best mushers we have."

He points to the low seat of the sled, lined with reindeer fur. "Kaiku can sit on your lap, Rory. Don't let her jump off."

I take my place in the basket obediently, tucking Mikkal's and my rucksacks in by my feet, and tying them in with some leathery rope ties that Rasmos shows me.

"You have to try later, though," Mikkal shouts, taking his standing position behind me at the back of the sled. "As musher! You can learn from me this first run!"

"They run in a formation of four. Ajax and Ona will lead, with Rocket and Upp directly behind them," Ivan says, coming up with three more dogs, getting them into position in their harnesses and hooking them to the sled.

"Ivan and I will ride on separate sleds, out in front," Jonne tells us. "The dogs will follow without instruction anyway."

He hands Mikkal one of the rifles. "We won't get separated," he tells him sternly. "But it makes sense we all carry one."

Kaiku clearly knows the drill and leaps into my lap, doing nose to tail circles until she finds a comfortable position to settle. I massage her neck, glad to have her familiar warmth against me for the ride.

There's a moment as we leave when I have this urge to scream stop, but it's gone in a flash, because we're off and the breath is whooshed out of me. Ajax and Ona first, Rocket and Upp just behind, straining on their harnesses, a blur of muted colours, snow flying up from their paws.

We whizz over the snow of the yard and out round the

now-familiar buildings of the settlement. I lean into the turn. The buildings pass in a haze, covered over in white now and surrounded by the ghostly shapes of the snow people – the last figures we see before we're out into the true wilderness.

Mikkal's laugh floats into the clear air and the ice wind whips past us. I pull my hat further down to cover my ears.

We pass a couple of reindeer, heads down in their familiar posture, their hooves kicking through the snow to find food. Their dark eyes look up to watch as we fly by.

Then Arctic foxes too, like Kaiku, except in their white winter colours. I only glimpse them at all because of their coal black noses and the rings around their eyes. One races us for a few moments, bounding alongside the sled, in and out of the snow, and Kaiku stands on my lap, ears alert, her pointed nose quivering.

"Hold on to her!" yells Mikkal from behind me. "Don't let her jump!" There's an edge of panic in his voice.

I wrap my mittened hands tighter round Kaiku's warm body and lean down to kiss the top of her head.

"You can't run wild today, little one," I whisper into her soft ears.

We watch her feral relative fall back as we overtake, further, faster, into the wintry landscape.

Our sled feels tiny and insignificant beside the mountains, which are set in tones of pink and violet, blushed with light. We fly past more reindeer, and ptarmigans, pecking at the ground.

"Easy! Whoa!" I hear from up ahead, and Mikkal starts repeating behind me. "Whoa!"

There's a reluctant slowing of the dogs, and something drags into the snow behind us as Mikkal pushes his foot into the brake pedal. The dogs whine in protest; they've barely begun, they're still hungry to be away.

"How was it, Rory? Did I do a good job?" Mikkal calls to me exuberantly.

"It felt like flying," I gush. "I've never gone so fast. I've never felt like that."

Mikkal grins proudly. "Isn't it the best feeling? We could get to the edge of the world if we kept going!"

Ahead, Jonne and Ivan have circled back with their sleds. They throw metal hooks into the snow, to anchor the dogs in place.

"We'll let the dogs rest a bit," Jonne informs us. "Stay by the sled, it'll be warmer."

Mikkal climbs in to sit on top of our rucksacks, opposite me. His brother hands each of us a flask of something hot and then starts fiddling with a portable stove.

"He's melting snow for the dogs," Mikkal explains. "Running makes them thirsty."

"I can't believe how fast they are." As if on cue, our leader, Ajax, appears by my side. He pushes his wet nose into my lap and Kaiku leaps off as if offended. She starts sniffing around Mikkal's flask instead.

"Ha!" he says. "This isn't for you, Kaiku!" He pushes her back towards me. "She won't be interested in yours, Rory. My mum made you some kind of meatless special."

"Really?" I say, unscrewing the top from my flask. The concoction of beans and vegetables in my hands smells amazing. "It's delicious," I say, starting to lap it up with relish. "Your mum's so kind."

"She likes you," Mikkal says, smiling. "She's happy I'm getting to meet new people."

"Will we see the mine soon?" I ask.

The distances don't make sense to me. The scale of everything is hard to gauge without the frames of reference I'm used to – roads, trees, houses.

"We'll loop back to the coast soon," Ivan says, overhearing. "We wanted to give the dogs a run inland first." He pats them affectionately.

"Rory's going to drive now," Mikkal tells him. I see Jonne looking over at his brother's words but he doesn't intervene.

My heart thuds against my ribs at the thought of being musher, yet I know I'll regret not trying it. Didn't I want to be brave here?

I let Ivan show me how to stand, where to grip the reins and where the brake pedal is, which operates the spikes that dig into the snow.

This time the dogs don't wait for the command to go, they're already off. It's a race, a flight, and through the ropes I feel all their wild impulses to run.

I'm panicked I'll fly head first and disappear, like Kaiku on one of her snowdives.

"You have to lean into the turns more, Rory!" Mikkal yells advice from in front of me, tucked in the basket under the reindeer skins.

"Whoa! Whoa!" I cry to the dogs, to try to get them to slow.

"Relax, Rory!" Mikkal's laughing now, and shouting in exhilaration, and then I am too. I've never had such a sense of freedom before. The power of the dogs at the end of the lines. The rush of our flight over the snow.

The muffled sky, the mountains, the blankness of the whole world. When the sled in front begins to slow, I'm surprised how disappointed I feel.

I slam my foot into the pedal and feel the brake grating against the snow. "Whoa! Whoa!"

We're somewhere else now. The landscape's shifted, like someone's taken a cross-section and we're seeing what's underneath.

"The new mine," Ivan announces. "This is the main site."

To our right is a sunken pit – a hollowed-out reverse

mountain in the tundra, cut down like orange skin unravelling. Except like the ptarmigans and the foxes, the mine too has taken on its winter camouflage. It's a snow-covered spiral.

The dogs yelp, anxious to be off again. I keep my tension on the ropes. Jonne and Ivan have already jumped off their sleds and hooked them firmly into the snow.

Mikkal jumps down too and goes over, but I stay with the dogs and Kaiku, who's curled up between our two rucksacks, out of the wind. Her eyes flicker. She's dreaming.

On the edge of the hollow, Jonne, Ivan and Mikkal look tiny. The mine is colossal, and strange and silent. A shiver runs through my body.

The landscape's growing blue as the sun sinks away. I look around, imagining for a moment I hear her voice. Ulya.

Can a ghost travel on a dog sled? If she's in my head, did I bring her with me? Or is she everywhere on Spitsbergen? What would she make of this new gash on the island?

"We're going to head north now," Mikkal tells me, coming back and rubbing his fingers together. "We'll keep close to the shoreline. From the map, Jonne thinks the most likely site for the tailings pond is a couple of hours away. And there's a cabin not far off where we'll stop for the night."

I stay silent. The sight of the mine makes me feel

disconnected from the three of them. This is what Mum came here to help make happen after all, and this cut into the tundra is only the start. I've seen the plans spread out before her, how they'll go wider. How they'll move from this site to another, and another.

"Rory!" Mikkal says again, irritated. "Did you listen to anything I just said?"

I nod quickly. "I'm just cold," I say, shivering now properly. My fingers are numb in my gloves from clutching the dog reins and the tip of my nose feels like it could drop off.

Mikkal's expression changes to concern. "Take a turn in the basket. I'll drive for the last part."

I climb gratefully into the scoop of the sled, glad of the warmth from the reindeer skins and Kaiku, who comes to nestle on my chest.

Mikkal takes the ropes and we go on, running our course over the snow, tracking beneath the stars and the green and ghostly aurora.

# Cabin

In the cabin, Ivan fiddles with an oil-powered lamp hanging down from the ceiling and a soft orange glow appears over us. Jonne's outside, sorting out the dogs. Mikkal is busy with a huge, ancient stove, arranging coal in the furnace from a stash in the corner and striking a match. I don't know how their fingers can work so fast. When I take my mittens off, my hands hurt like they've been burned.

On two sides of the room are sets of bunks at right angles to each other – four beds in total. Another wall has a shelf with pans hanging from it and various battered tins of food.

"Cod roe, mackerel, liver pate, fish balls…" Mikkal translates the tin labels for me, when he's got the fire going. "Ah, these might be OK for you, Rory. Mixed vegetables, and peach slices? But it's good Mum cooked for you, I think!"

I nod gratefully in agreement. I've sunk on to a bench, still wrapped in the reindeer hide from the sled. Kaiku is sleeping in my arms like a hot water bottle. I wish I could sleep too – the exposure of being out on the sled, and finally seeing the mine, has zapped all my energy.

"Come closer to the fire, Rory," Jonne instructs, coming inside. "You got cold! Your lips are blue!"

I move forwards obediently. The flames are crackling in the stove now, warm and inviting. Smoke billows out into the room and Ivan arranges the metal pans over the stove and empties a couple of the cans into them.

"Who puts the food here?" I ask, curious at how well-stocked the cabin is, despite being so many miles from the town.

"We keep them maintained," Ivan says. "It's in case anyone gets lost out here. They are a survival line." He wafts a particularly black cloud of smoke away with an irritated hand and gives a gruff laugh. "This chimney needs fixing. Greenlight distracted us, this summer."

We eat from metal bowls. I have heated-up vegetables – peas, cabbage and carrots in a briny liquid – and the rest of the stew Mikkal's mum had prepared especially for me, reheated to piping hot. Afterwards we open the peaches, which are oversweet and soft, but which we all devour anyway, knowing our bodies need the fuel to stay warm.

No one talks very much – everyone's tired after being

out for so long in the cold – but Jonne and Ivan discuss the different options for where the tailings pond might be. They've identified a few possible places from the maps I showed them.

"What will it look like?" Mikkal asks.

Jonne shrugs, his dark eyes lost in the firelight. I wonder if he's thinking about Pia.

"We'll know it when we see it," Ivan answers beside him. His eyes flick across to me.

I keep staring into the flames. As much as I want us to find the tailings site, I'm also dreading it. I'm worried it'll be too big a barrier to cross, between me and the people of Pyramiden.

# Wilderness

I wake to Mikkal snoring in the bunk beneath me.

The walls of the hut glisten in the yellow lamplight. The fire's melted away the layer of ice that had frozen over them.

It's still dark outside, but it must be morning. Kaiku's scrabbling at the door and I can hear the dogs whining in a separate lean-to.

"We need to let them out," Jonne says, his voice making me jump. He's sweeping out the ashes from the stove and his hands are smudged black.

Ivan's still asleep, across from me at the top of the second set of bunks.

"We always leave the hut as before," Jonne explains to me. "For the next people, whoever they may be."

Hearing our voices, the dogs get louder, and Kaiku

jumps up at my legs excitedly. Ivan stirs and stretches his arms out. "Morning, Rory. How are you feeling? You did well yesterday, as musher."

Pride spreads through me remembering the feeling of the day before, flying through the snow, the connection with the dogs through the ropes. I push the vision of the mine away.

"You can let them out if you like," Jonne says, indicating the dogs next door.

"Won't they run away?"

Jonne gives a slight smile. "Not before they've eaten. I'll send Mikkal out with food and water." He shakes his brother awake to tired groans.

The dogs sniff around excitedly when I let them out, clearly pleased to see a human. They follow me as I walk towards a shore, a little bit in front of the cabin. We're next to a fjord.

"I'm sorry I don't have food for you," I tell the dogs, as they swirl round my legs, noses twitching. "Mikkal's coming soon with your meat! I promise!"

The morning darkness is different here, away from any buildings except the tiny wooden cabin. You really experience the twilight – the sun still sunk below the horizon but casting a strange half-light. On the shore are more of the ghost trees, and arches of porous white whale bones and reindeer antlers. Things melt into each other and the boulders on the shore could almost be mountains.

Something flies over my shoulder and hits the ice by the water's edge. I jump round quickly but it's just Mikkal. He's thrown a stone from behind me. The dogs flock to bowls of meat in front of the cabin.

"How was your first night in the true wilderness?" Mikkal asks me.

"I survived," I say with a shiver. The air is the sharpest I've experienced yet, and I think longingly of the hot water back in our block in Pyramiden, the fifty per cent of the time the boiler decides to work.

"Mikkal! Rory!" Jonne shouts. "Come and eat! We need to pack up the sleds soon. There might be a storm coming. We want to find this site while we have the chance."

I'm musher again as we set back out on to the snowy tundra. Today I'm braver, better, faster. We fly across the snow, and past a bear that's just a yellow smudge on the horizon.

"Polar bear!" I yell into the wind, part of me wishing we could double back to see it, part of me feeling enormous relief that we've left it behind. I know I'll carry that encounter on the mountainside to my grave.

The wind picks up as we travel. Icier, now. Little stabs of pain against your face. But we go on, past more foxes and ptarmigans, and reindeer too, which look at us with sorrowful eyes, as if urging us to go faster.

"Kaiku!" Mikkal screams suddenly from the sled. "Stop! Stop!" He swings his face round wildly. "Stop them, Rory! Kaiku! I lost her!"

I stare at the dogs' feet, the thrown-up snow, Jonne and Ivan flying on before us. How on earth do I stop Ajax and her team now?

"Rory!" Tears freeze on Mikkal's face. "Stop!"

I try and make out the adults ahead – blue-grey shapes disappearing in the swirling whiteness. We've driven into the storm.

"Rory!" Mikkal shouts. "Your foot! Brake!"

I try my right foot on the metal bar. The tension on the ropes increases, but the dogs continue flying forwards. They're trained to follow the sled in front. They're not expecting additional commands from me, I realize.

"Rory!" Mikkal shouts crossly now. "Harder!"

I transfer all my weight to my right foot, slamming the bar down to the bottom of the sled to press the metal spikes of the brake into the ice and snow.

"Whoa! Whoa!" Mikkal is shouting at the huskies, both more masterly and more desperately than me, or maybe it's the brake that makes the difference. The dogs pull themselves to a reluctant stop.

"Jonne! Ivan!" I call at the top of my voice, panicked. Our dogs yelp at being separated from the rest of their pack.

Mikkal's oblivious. He bounds out of the basket and

runs back along the tracks of the sled.

"What are you doing? Mikkal!"

"Kaiku jumped off! She went after a ptarmigan."

"Mikkal, they've gone on without us," I say, properly scared now. The noise of our four dogs picks up. Ajax starts howling. "We've lost them!"

Kaiku's built small and ready to survive. She belongs here so absolutely, but if we lose Jonne and Ivan, what will happen to us?

"They'll turn around as soon as they realize," Mikkal says indifferently. "Jonne's got a sixth sense in the snow." He's still moving back along our sled tracks, calling Kaiku's name frantically.

Visibility is just a few metres, less, and I jump off the sled too, to be closer to Mikkal, terrified of being left alone with just the dogs for company in the snowy wilderness. They've grown more like wolves since we set off. As beautiful as ever but so wild they frighten me.

"Where can she have gone?" Mikkal says. I've never heard fear in his voice before, but he loves that fox to bits.

I gesture into the nothingness of the blizzard. Kaiku could be anywhere. Even with her blue-grey fur, in these conditions, she'd disappear. "You should have put her on a lead or something," I say, frustrated. Who knows how far ahead Jonne and Ivan are now? Have they even noticed we've stopped following?

Mikkal looks at me with irritation. "A lead! Kaiku's a wild animal."

"So why did you make me stop the sled for her? Can't she take care of herself?"

Mikkal opens his mouth to riposte back to me, but his face freezes in horror. "The dogs, Rory."

"The dogs," I repeat, turning round slowly.

There's nothing there.

In front of me is pure wind and snow. The whining and the chime of the bells on the dogs' collars have gone away.

Mikkal and I stare at each other helplessly, the terrible realization dawning on us.

"What do we do?" I voice, but Mikkal only continues to stare at me, fear widening his eyes.

"Mikkal!" I say, shaking him.

Standing still is the worst thing we could do. We'll become like the snow people that are taking over the square.

Something hurls into my legs – a soft grey ripple of fur.

"Kaiku!" Mikkal announces, gathering her up into his arms with relief. "You came back!" She tries to burrow her way into his coat. She's whining, scared. "It's OK," Mikkal says, making soft petting noises.

I look up to the sky, for Polaris or the moon, or anything, anything at all to orientate us. All there is is snow.

"What do we do?" I shout.

"Jonne will turn around for us. He'll follow the tracks."

We stare at the ground, at the falling snow. Our tracks are already gone, the wind has blown over them.

"We could walk in that direction, forwards?" Mikkal says. "We can't stay still. We'll freeze!"

Is it forwards? I look in the direction he's pointing. We're directionless now.

It's darker too. We fumble independently for torches in our deep pockets.

Neither of us speaks the absolute horror we're feeling as we start to walk. Hypothermia, bears, the utter darkness of the polar night.

There's a noise ahead. Not really a voice, but a presence, and a prickling sensation around my head.

"Did you hear that?" I ask sharply.

Mikkal swings round, alarmed. He shines his light into my face.

"There's someone ahead. Something," I say, unsure how I put into words what I hear, or feel, or know. Something in the darkness, off to the side of us.

Mikkal's eyes are wide and questioning.

"Are those footprints?" I ask, gritting my teeth to control their chattering, directing my torch at some rough marks in the snow.

Mikkal shakes his head uneasily.

"It could be tracks, from the others," I offer.

"It's not dog sleds," he says emphatically.

"Footmarks then. Snow boots. They could have got off to look for us on foot. That makes sense, doesn't it? Jonne could have. He would have!" I insist.

"What if it's a bear?" Mikkal says.

"Even I can see they're not bear tracks," I say, except as I look at them, I realize I can't be sure of anything.

I hear the noise again. Close by, and off to the side, in the direction of the tracks in the snow, that may not even be tracks, or may be the tracks of a polar bear that is already stalking us. I hold my gloved hand up to my ear, to try and get a better sense of what it is that I'm hearing.

Mikkal looks on nervously.

"It's like a voice. Calling our names," I say. "Do you hear it? Listen, Mikkal!" I plead with him to hear it too.

Mikkal leans in closer, his breath on my face. Kaiku has disappeared into his coat now.

"I can't hear anything except the blizzard," he cries back.

"It could be Jonne," I venture, even though I know it isn't. This voice is higher, younger. Ulya.

*Mikkal! Rory!*

"We have to follow it," I say.

Mikkal shakes his head uneasily, looking at me with a flicker of terror, as though he doesn't quite trust me. I read about something called *Ishavet kaller* in that book back in Longyearbyen, about the hunters and trappers of Svalbard. It's a strangeness that can come over people in the Arctic winter. Trappers walked out into the snowy wastes to their deaths or threw themselves into the sea. It's a kind of madness, the book said.

*Mikkal! Rory!* I hear again, calling us on, to keep walking.

Mikkal reads the noises in my face. He's resigned himself to whatever strange thing has taken over me. He knows if we stay still, we're dead anyway.

# Blizzard

We bend into the wind, blunder forwards. One foot after another, this is the way you walk through a blizzard. We'll crawl on all fours if we need to.

If you die trapped in a blizzard in Spitsbergen, are you there forever, endlessly putting one foot in front of another and another? Would we even realize we'd died? Is that what it's like for Ulya, running through the corridors of her old building, soaring high into the air on the swing?

My eyelids are freezing shut. It's a conscious effort every time I blink to reopen them.

I envy Mikkal for the little bundle of warmth on his chest, even if Kaiku is the reason we're out here at all, and not safe in the hut already, with a roaring fire and yellow oil light.

Someone is still ahead of us. Or something. There are

footprints, but the blizzard obscures them, and I can't work out whether it's another person, or whether they're our own tracks and we're going round in circles.

I know it's not Jonne and Ivan we're following. I've lost every rational sense in my body apart from its ability to feel the cold. The noises at night, the unseen shadows through the corridors of Building Nine, Paris, maybe they've been leading me here, to the darkness at the heart of Svalbard.

Ice, all around us. An explosion of it far up in the sky. Ice and snow crystals in our ears and nose and eyes.

The wind's from the end of the world itself with its blades of ice and I worry suddenly about crevasses, like on the glacier. That we could step into nothing.

I'm at the point of despair when I spot something ahead. A building. A hut, like the one we stayed in last night. At first I think it's my hypothermic brain, conjuring it up from utter desperation, but Mikkal must see it too, because his snow stumble regains a purpose. A man-made structure, in the middle of the wilderness. Shelter.

The hut is further than it looks. We blunder on and it doesn't get closer for ages. But finally we're pushing together against the door, kicking snow away desperately with our feet. With our combined weight, we manage to force it open. Mikkal holds the door as the wind wrestles to take it away and I squeeze in past him.

There's a tiny space, barely big enough for one person, like a little hallway. Usually you'd leave your boots here and take off your coats, but Mikkal and I slam the door behind us, and push forwards into the next space.

"Jonne! Jonne!" Mikkal calls hopefully, certain his brother will be here waiting for him. There's no answer. We flash our torches around an empty space.

This hut's smaller than yesterday's. There's just one set of bunks against a wall and a metal stove with a tall, dark chimney that goes up into the roof. There are a few hooks and shelves, mostly empty, though I register with relief a few cans of food. We won't starve at least.

"Wood," Mikkal whispers, spotting a pile in the corner. He builds a stack of wood in the stove and reaches under his coat for a little parcel. I watch his frozen fingers unwrap a piece of waxy cloth to reveal a small box of matches.

He strikes one and it sparks into flame immediately. Mikkal throws it into the stove and uses a metal fork next to the grate to prod at the wood as he blows the fire to life.

I cry with relief at the miraculous synergy of light and warmth.

I notice some reindeer skins on one of the bottom bunks and drag them over to the fire. We hang our wet coats and overtrousers on some hooks to dry.

Only when we're safely in our cocoon of reindeer hides in front of the fire does Kaiku climb out from Mikkal's jumper. She eyes us suspiciously.

"You damn fox," Mikkal says with conviction. "You almost got us killed."

Kaiku blinks sweetly. Outside the wind roars.

"I'm sorry, Rory," Mikkal whispers into the fire.

I shake my head.

"I panicked," he goes on. "I should never have left you with the dogs. It was only your second time as musher. You were doing great!"

"I let them go," I say miserably. "The main thing I had to do was keep hold of them, and I let them go."

Mikkal squeezes my hand. "They should be better trained. Stupid dogs. They're no better than wolves!"

I laugh softly. The fire crackles as it dances in the draught from the stovepipe and sometimes threatens to go out as particularly vicious gusts come down into the room. "Do you think they'll be OK? What if they're lost too?" I ask, my mind still on Ajax and the others.

"Huskies are bred to survive out here. They'll be just fine."

We lapse into silence, listening to the wind moaning eerily, as the snow banks up outside.

"Will Jonne find us, do you think?" I ask, a new edge of desperation in my voice as night approaches. "This is the same hut he was heading to?"

"It must be," Mikkal says assuredly. "Jonne will come tomorrow."

I know from the fear in his eyes that he's lying. He's never been here before.

# Dream

I dream of ice and darkness and falling through crevasses into freezing water.

There's a huge shadow in the depths. A bowhead or a Greenland shark.

"Rory, Rory!" Mikkal is tugging at my shoulder to wake me. "You're dreaming!"

My eyes can't focus on his face in the dark. For a moment I'm back in Dad's hut, in the forest. Branches tapping on the roof, the chattering of crows overhead, woodsmoke, safety.

Then I shiver. All the warmth in my imagining dies. We've fallen asleep by the fire.

"You were whimpering," Mikkal complains.

"I'm sorry," I say, through chattering teeth. Kaiku stirs between us then resettles back to sleep, curling up tighter.

I stumble over to the stove to throw more wood on the fire. How long does a pile of wood last in a wilderness? What will happen if Jonne and Ivan don't come tomorrow?

Or maybe it's tomorrow already. It's not like when we first arrived on Spitsbergen. The mornings aren't distinguishable now; it takes so long for the sun to rise at all. I peer through the black square of window. If I could see Polaris, the North Star, it would be like Dad was watching over me, but the sky's still clouded up with snow.

"What was it last night, do you think?" Mikkal whispers. "Out there."

"Did you hear her?" I ask quickly, scrutinizing his face. Last night I definitely got the impression Mikkal didn't want to talk about it.

"Her?" he asks, puzzled.

I swallow nervously. "I think it's her. Jonne's friend. I think it's Ulya, Mikkal."

Mikkal stares at me strangely. "That was why you wanted me to look through the photos with you, wasn't it? For a ghost?"

"She led me up there. I think she wanted to tell me who she was. Show me."

I can't work out Mikkal's expression in the dim light, whether it's fear or disbelief or something else.

"She doesn't want to do us harm," I whisper. "She wanted to help. She's become like a friend to me. I think she knew I was lonely. In the beginning."

"I'm sorry, Rory," Mikkal whispers. "It wasn't because we didn't like you. It was because…"

"I was with Greenlight," I say, picking the final words for him.

Mikkal nods slowly. "It was still no reason to be like that. Not to you. My mum was right, we never needed to be enemies."

A smile creeps on to my face, thinking of Mikkal's mum. Her face when she saw my pictures of Dad's woodland.

"You should have listened to your fox," I tell Mikkal lightly. "Kaiku knew from the beginning I was worth being friends with."

Mikkal groans. "Don't mention her! I've still not forgiven her for getting us lost. If it wasn't for Ulya we'd have frozen to death out there!"

# Exposure

When the blizzard stops, Mikkal and I put our coats back on and push the door against the weight of the banked-up snow. It takes all of our strength to open it.

We're by a shallow stretch of water, where a new fjord has been carved out of the tundra. But this one isn't pewter grey like the natural landscape of Spitsbergen; this is dirty orange and yellow. It's covered in a blackened crust and frost circles it too, as if Svalbard is doing its best to cover it over, only it's not done a very good job.

The tailings pond, it has to be. This is what's left, after Greenlight's prize earth metals have been blown out with acid and chemicals. It's what they denied existed.

Discarded to one side, monstrous against the snow, is an orange construction vehicle. And then, at the edge of the huge pool, half covered in snow, are the bodies of six or seven reindeer.

"We found it," Mikkal breathes.

When the ice melts, it'll all spill out further into the fjords, killing the fish and seals, the walrus and whales.

I stumble forwards. "This is where Ulya led us," I whisper, knowing I'm right. She gained my trust so she could show me this place. Did she know where it was all along?

I put out my hand, imagining I might feel her fingertips on mine through my frosted gloves. Or see her face staring out of the ice, blinking in recognition. But Ulya's not here. This place is empty of any life. Even the air feels dead and poisoned.

Mikkal stands staring at it all, holding Kaiku tightly in his arms to keep her from it. "How can they do this? They don't care, any of those people. They get what they want out of the earth and then they leave again. Even Pia did. Jonne's right. They're no better than the whalers." He spits into the snow and stares back at me, his eyes wide and distrustful in the dim light.

"Pia hadn't seen this," I say certainly, picturing her on the glacier that day. "She hadn't seen this or she would have been shouting about it."

Mikkal shrugs hopelessly.

"I think it was Pia who deleted my mum's report," I tell him. "For your brother, and for this place. And for my mum too."

Mikkal glances at me in surprise.

"To stop her making such a terrible mistake," I say.

Mikkal grunts. "Your mum must have suspected this was happening. She must have done, Rory."

I shake my head. On Mum's trips with Mark and the others, they can't have brought her here, can they? She can't have seen this place and still thought the mine was OK.

Certainly not the reindeer. Mikkal passes Kaiku to me and then goes right up to them, bending down to their level.

I wrap my arms round Kaiku. Usually she'd be straining to be free but today she's content being held.

I will the reindeer to get to their feet and race away, like the ones around the town. Wired and skittish, ready to run the moment they sense danger. These creatures can outrun polar bears and survive freezing dark winters. They're built to survive. They shouldn't be dying like this, at the edge of a slurry pond.

There's a quiver behind Mikkal and the smallest reindeer raises her head, her black eyes searching us out intensely. Does she think we've come to help her? It must be her mother lying dead beside her.

Mikkal strokes the neck of the little creature, tears smudging with earth and dust on his face as he speaks to her. I wonder what he's saying. Mikkal's used to death and hunting as a way of life, but this is different. This kind of sickness.

I'm aware more than ever of the phone in my pocket and the lights and air conditioning and heating in Mum's and my apartment back home. All of the modern world and our appliances and conveniences. "We need to tell people about this." I sniff.

"What people? The Greenlight people? Your mum? They know, Rory. They did it. They're part of it. Jonne was right. We shouldn't have trusted any of you." He throws the words out across the ice.

"You're wrong," I say, certain now. "About my mum. I know her. If she sees this, she'll do something. The Arctic Council too. It's their job to protect this place."

"They look away if they're paid enough, like Jonne says."

"That's why we need evidence then, for when we get back." I try to turn my phone on but it's totally dead. The battery's gone, or the cold has made it short circuit or something.

"They won't listen to us anyway. We don't matter to them," Mikkal says dully.

"They'll have to listen now we've found the site. We can show them pictures of it," I insist. "People like my mum and Pia. They came out here to do a job in an amazing place. They don't want to be part of its destruction. And the Arctic Council are about to make their final visit. They can't ignore this."

Mikkal looks across at the yellow strap round my neck. "You think that thing will work out here?"

"It's worth a try. It worked on the glacier, didn't it? I've had it close to my body, to keep it as warm as possible."

Mikkal stays beside the reindeer as I walk around the pond.

I only have one last box of film with me, five little squares of photo. I have to make them count. I stand back to take a couple with as much of the site as I can get in, with the position of the real fjord to the west of us, and the construction vehicle and sections of pipe, covered over in snow. I put the flash on for extra light. Then I move on to the reindeer, taking a couple of shots of the whole group, and finishing with the smallest one. Her gumline is discoloured and her eyes are opaque and yellow.

"Do you think they will be enough?" Mikkal asks.

"It's proof of something," I say, filled with determination now. "Whatever they might say it is, they definitely can't say it's nothing. The Arctic Council will have to come and see for themselves."

Mikkal gives the reindeer one last stroke and walks back to me.

Something has clicked in my brain taking the photos. There's a new clarity. "I think I know where we are," I say.

The hut, the shape of the bay, the mountains opposite. "It's not where Jonne and Ivan were heading, but it was marked on the map, this place, with a cross," I tell him.

"So it's not another feeling?" Mikkal asks reluctantly. "Or Ulya again?"

"Not this time. If I'm right," I continue, gulping, "it means we came further west than Jonne intended. The other cabins would be north of here. If we followed the line of the shore, we could find them. Catch up with them."

Mikkal stares at me, wondering if he should trust me. He knows we'll only have a couple of hours of light at most. "Rory, if we walk further north and you're wrong…" He leaves the consequences unsaid and looks back to the cabin.

He sighs. "We should at least eat first. Some of those battered cans must have something vegetarian for you." He pauses. "And then we'll go. You're right. We have to show someone our evidence."

# Rescue

I don't have Ulya on my side today, whispering into my ear, calling me forwards. But Mikkal and I both feel a new purpose as we set out. We've found the tailings pond that Andrèi and Mark went to such lengths to keep hidden.

"They'll be furious with you, Rory," Mikkal says as we walk. He looks older than his years, with his gun slung over his shoulder.

"Laura's daughter," I say, mocking Mark's voice. "They underestimated me. And you, Mikkal."

He gives a smile of satisfaction. The snow is thick here and our feet sink right into it. The sun is above the horizon for one of the last days of light before the true polar night, and all around is swan white, beautiful. It's good for our eyes, after seeing the mine sites. This is what Svalbard should be. This is how I want to remember it.

Kaiku's in her element, bounding up and down beside us through the snow, like a ripple of water.

We hear the dogs before we see the cabin, a thin trail of smoke spiralling out from it into the already darkening sky. Relief sparks in my chest.

Jonne's outside, loading up a sled. He runs forwards when he sees our torches.

Mikkal throws himself into his brother's arms.

I hang back, counting the dim shadows of the dogs, pleased to see they all made it here.

Ajax appears at my side, brushing sheepishly against my legs. "You left us!" I admonish, wrapping my arms round him, planting tears on his fur.

"We've been out looking for hours. We were just about to set out the other way. We thought we'd lost you for good!" Jonne's saying to Mikkal. He's trembling and his eyes look wide and frightened at what might have been. He's already lost too many people in his life.

"It was my fault," I step in. "I was a terrible musher. I let go of the dogs."

"No, Rory," Mikkal interrupts loyally. "We know who was to blame. It was my disobedient fox!"

As if in answer, Kaiku pokes her pointed nose out of Mikkal's coat and jumps down to the dogs.

"Well, bring them in!" Ivan shouts from the door of the cabin, coming out to greet us and pulling us both into a warm hug. "We thought that was it for you two, out in that blizzard. Where on earth did you spend the night?"

Inside, Mikkal launches into the news of the cabin we found and the tailings pond and the reindeer. I pass round the square pictures I took and watch Jonne and Ivan exchange glances, a mixture of horror and relief in their faces. The Arctic Council can't ignore something has happened here now. We can lead them right to the site.

"We could go back and show you," I offer, but Ivan shakes his head fervently.

"Your mum will be worried, Rory. We need to get the two of you home. And I need to get back to my Nina. She doesn't like me being away."

We don't waste any time before setting off. Jonne and Ivan are mushers. Mikkal travels with his brother; I don't think Jonne will let him out of his sight for a while. I go with Ivan and the third sled trails behind ours, threatening to escape every dip and peak of the snowy landscape we travel over.

It's hard to keep my eyes from closing. The cold and fear from being out in the blizzard has caught up with me. I know if it hadn't been for Ulya, there's no way we'd have made it out of there. And however hard Jonne and Ivan looked for us, in those conditions it would have been too late.

I can't ever let Mum know all the things I experienced

last night. She's too rational, she'll blame herself for making me hallucinate. But one day, I'll try telling Dad about it. He did say he wanted to know everything about my Svalbard adventure.

I'm woken by voices. Shouts, barking, commotion. I force my eyes open, brushing ice from my eyelashes. Another sled has come up beside us. Rasmos. He's calling our names excitedly. "We were getting worried. You have Rory with you, yes? Her mum's distraught. Nina too, Ivan."

I sit up straighter, desperate now for Mum, and to be properly warm. Ivan and Jonne take the sleds all the way into the square.

Mum's standing outside the Cultural Palace with Mikkal's mum and Nina, the three of them united in worry. They surge forwards together. Mikkal and I barely wait for the sleds to slow and we're off, our feet pounding into the snow.

Mum gathers me up in her arms. "Rory, my darling. I was so worried when the snowstorm started…"

"Mum, Mum," I cry, unable to summon up any words beside that. She pulls me inside. I'm dimly aware of Greenlight employees – Mark, Ingrid, some of the engineers, and Jonne's raised voice. Ivan's too, even as he buries himself in a hug with his daughter. They're shouting, they must be telling them what Mikkal and I found.

Mum's expression is confused. "Rory, what are they

saying? What did you see out there?"

Someone's handing out hot drinks and I clutch one gratefully. Mum leads me to a sofa. Not my hidden one, beneath the staircase, but part of a group by a heater, where Mikkal's mum is smothering him with kisses.

"I have photos. Jonne has them. Mum, we found another site. A waste pond. There were dead reindeer all around it."

"What do you mean?"

"Like they told us, Mum. It's what poisoned the reindeer."

Mum's face collapses. "You're not talking about the mine itself?"

I shake my head. "No, we saw that too. This was north of there." I give a scrambled explanation of what we found, and Mikkal chips in to elaborate.

"They lied to me," Mum keeps repeating, and I'm glad Mikkal and Nina are both here to see her devastation as the scale of Greenlight's cover-up becomes clear to everyone.

At first Mark sticks around and tries to pass it off as an early error, a harmless blunder, but a couple of the engineers contradict him, and soon Mark disappears. Andrei never comes at all. It's Mum who's suddenly in control of things.

I sink back into the sofa, still covered in one of the reindeer hides, as she makes plans with Ivan and Jonne to be taken to the tailings pond tomorrow with the delegates from the Arctic Council. The *Leviathan* is bringing them in the morning.

I'm dozing off again when Mum shakes me. "Rory, are you ready to come back to Paris? Ingrid's run a hot bath for you."

"The boiler's on?" I say incredulously.

Mum smiles. "Luck's on your side. Hot bath and bed. You've done well today." She laughs sadly. "You've done well since we got here." She pulls me to my feet and rearranges the reindeer skin around me. Mikkal's already disappeared, back to his apartment to sleep, I suppose. Mum and I walk across the frozen square together and her arm doesn't leave my shoulder once.

# Ghost

It's our final day on Spitsbergen. Jonne's at the kennels, where Mikkal told me I'd find him. I can't leave without telling him about what I heard, or felt, or experienced, that day in the blizzard. Whatever it was. I owe that to her. To Ulya.

He nods as I approach, almost as if he's been expecting me. I lean over the gate, my hands dropping into the warm softness of the dogs as they leap up noisily to greet me. I'm silent for a moment, wondering how to tell him a thing like that. That I think I've been visited by the ghost of his dead best friend. That she might have saved my life, and Mikkal's too.

It's Jonne who starts to speak. "You did a good job, Rory. I couldn't get them to listen to me but you, you found a way."

I nod. There's been a suspension of operations on the island, and a thorough investigation ordered for late spring, when the snow melts. Andrei and Mark have already left. Tomorrow Mum and I leave too, along with most of the engineers. Our time on Spitsbergen is almost up. "Thank you for taking me to the whaling station. I think I needed that push, to fully believe what was happening here."

Jonne laughs softly. "Did you think that was just for your benefit?"

I raise my eyebrows uncertainly. "You were angry with me, for being part of it all." I pause. "I don't blame you."

Jonne sighs. "Whatever it was I thought I was doing that day, well, it wasn't really for you, Rory."

Suddenly it falls into place. "It was for her, wasn't it? For Pia?"

Jonne squeezes a smile. "I was trying to get her to change her mind."

I bend my head to the side.

"I was sure she knew about the tailings pond, even though she insisted she didn't," Jonne goes on, his face pained. "I should just have trusted her more. You saw Pia at the glacier. How much she loves this place."

"Yes," I say quietly. "She adored it." It shone through her. I feel certain now that Pia deleted Mum's report, to buy this place more time.

Jonne shuffles his feet in the snow. "My mum is right.

Growing up here, you don't learn how to be around other people. No wonder Pia left. I wasn't worth hanging around for. I don't deserve her." He looks wretched, standing there, though Ajax is licking his fingers and staring at him devotedly. Jonne lifts his chin. "Mikkal is better than me. I'm glad the two of you became friends."

"Pia liked you so much," I say, the words coming out in a rush. "You made her happy. I know you did. It wasn't you she was leaving, Jonne, it was Pyramiden. And Andrei and Mark."

Jonne's eyes flicker in acknowledgement. "This place can be terrifying sometimes. It has its ghosts."

I stare back for a moment, shivering in the cold air. Then I take a deep breath and tell him about the footsteps I heard in the corridors of Paris. The face in the mirror. The singing. How sometimes she called my name. Jonne listens intently without saying anything.

"Did you leave me a book about whaling?" I ask, remembering back to my first days here. "Outside my room?"

He shakes his head. "Do you know who that book belonged to, Rory?"

Icy air travels down my windpipe. "It was your friend's. It was Ulya's," I say, knowing the answer at once, as surely as if her name had been printed in the front, in her neat capitals.

Jonne nods. "Someone must have brought it here. Some naturalist or tourist, or maybe some miner even. She found it in our little library. Ulya couldn't get over everything that had happened to the whales here. She knew the fjords would still be swimming with them, if it hadn't been for people."

"You drew them for her, didn't you? Those whales in my room? Mikkal said you used to draw." I can see it in my mind's eye as I say it. The two of them on the beach by the whaling station. Ulya pointing out the magnificent creatures while Jonne sketched them quickly, before his fingers got too cold.

Jonne laughs quietly. "Of all the rooms to pick for you, Pia picked Ulya's. She had no idea what she was doing. What she started."

"You don't think I made her up then?" I say, my heart lurching, realizing how important it is to me that someone else believes in her.

"I don't think you made her up, Rory."

"When I came here, I'd been lonely. I'd been lonely for ages. I think Ulya wanted me to have a friend," I offer.

Jonne runs his fingers through his hair. "I was lonely too. Then this summer, when Greenlight came and started excavating again, something changed."

"Pia," I whisper.

Jonne nods slowly. "I realized I'd stopped hearing Ulya.

She'd gone away. I felt guilty that I'd betrayed her, even though it was time, maybe. It had been enough years." He hesitates. "I'm glad she found you, Rory."

"What was she like?" I ask.

Jonne's eyes swim with memories. "Ulya was obsessed with the whales. She adored them. She'd walk the shores searching for them, and sit on the mountainside, looking out towards the glacier. Her mum always worried a bear would come and take her." He laughs gently. "I'd go with her, to draw, and because she was just such a good person to be around. She made me laugh. We had so much fun together."

I smile, imagining their friendship. It felt like that with Betty, I think. I reckon you're always lucky, to find a friend like that.

Jonne swallows loudly. "It should have been me that day, by the mines. I should have been the one taking my dad his lunch. I was drawing and lost track of time. Mum was busy with Mikkal. Ulya was passing and told Mum she'd go instead."

His voice quivers with sadness. "She was just fifteen, Rory. She'd barely lived. She hated that mine too. She hated the dark, she was always searching out the light. And that's where she was buried…"

"No," I say, gripped with urgency now. "She's not there any more. That's what I came to tell you. That day, in the blizzard, Ulya was with us, Jonne, with me and Mikkal. She showed us to the cabin by the tailings pond. I thought it was because she wanted to show me the reindeer, so I could see what the mine is doing to this place, but it was to save Mikkal too, I think. To save him for you."

"Ulya was with you out there?" Jonne gestures to the snowy fields outside of town.

I nod firmly. "She saved us."

Jonne closes his eyes for a few seconds. I look down at Ajax who has moved over to me, pushing his nose into my gloves as if to comfort me, or find some stray snack.

"Tell me, Rory, do you still hear her?" Jonne asks quietly.

"No." I pause. "Not since that day. Maybe she knows neither of us needs her any more. And she knows the reindeer and the whales will be safe now."

Jonne exhales slowly and wipes a tear away. "Mikkal thinks we should leave this place. Take the Arctic Council up on their offer of housing back in Finland. They're talking about giving subsistence hunting rights, for the reindeer. The herds are bigger there. Mikkal could go to school, get a proper education." He looks up at me.

"You sound like my mum!" I joke.

"Then your mum is right. You *should* have opportunities," Jonne says sternly. "You young people. You should have options, to live the kind of life you want to live."

I imagine Mikkal in a vast pine forest, seeing the way the light filters through the trees and flowers burst up from the ground in spring. I imagine him going to school, hungry to learn and make new friends.

I hold Jonne's gaze. "You should live the kind of life you want to live too. You can't go on blaming yourself, just because you didn't take your dad lunch one day when you were fifteen years old. Blame the mining company. Or blame this place. I don't think you should blame yourself."

He laughs hollowly. "I couldn't leave them all. Dad, Ulya. My brothers."

"I don't think that's what Ulya would want," I say, filled with new boldness. "You staying here because you felt obliged to. She'd want you to be happy. And if your dad was anything like mine, he'd want you to be happy too."

I reach into my pocket, to the little envelope where I have the rest of the photos. The ones the Arctic Council don't need as evidence and that haven't made it into my journal yet. I've been using up all the film I have the last couple of days, knowing I'll never come anywhere like this ever again.

The Cultural Palace and the empty swimming pool and my own room, Ulya's room, with its metal bed and a wall full of whales. Then outside, the reindeer and ptarmigans on the slopes. And beautiful blue Kaiku. I could fill a whole book with photos of her.

I find the one I took of Jonne and Pia on the glacier. "This is for you," I say, handing it to him.

Jonne stares at the little square photo. "We look happy," he comments, almost like it's a surprise. Did he not see it that day? It felt like they were meant to be together.

I press it into his hand firmly.

"You've done a good job with your photos here, Rory."

"I took them so I can remember," I tell him fiercely. "I want to remember every single thing here forever."

Svalbard is what I'll think of, on bad days at school, when I feel I don't fit in, or that I'm trapped in a town with not enough space to breathe. I'll come in my head to a rocky island in the middle of the Arctic Ocean, in the approach to winter when it only gets light a couple of hours a day, but my head was flooded with it.

# Home

In the dock, like a great sea monster herself, the *Leviathan* waits to take us home.

Jonne and Mikkal pass our bags up, and I hug them goodbye. Jonne shyly and awkwardly, and then Mikkal tight and tearfully. Then the others come, the full crowd of them, and I embrace each of them in turn. Nina's slightly cautious. "I wish we had more time, to become friends," I say, still with my new boldness. I don't want to regret anything here.

Nina smiles. "We had fun that day, in the snow fight."

I nod happily. I know it will be one of my favourite memories here.

I save my last hug for Kaiku, almost squeezing the life out of her. She looks at me oddly. Her pointed little face has no idea of the significance of the moment.

"I'll miss you," I laugh through my tears, kissing her wet nose one last time.

Mum and I stand on the stern, waving goodbye, as the townspeople turn to leave. It's too cold to wait, except for Mikkal, who stays for ages, his bright voice travelling through the clear air. "Farewell, Rory! I'll see you in a forest some day!"

The *Leviathan* heaves herself through the water. The ice is forming in earnest now, and the captain is intent at the wheel, to steer his passage through the floes. I sit quietly on the deck, hanging over the edge, watching.

"The polar night was too much for you?" the captain asks after a while, a twinkle in his eye.

"No," I say, my voice sharp and certain. "It's just time for us to go home now. My dad will be missing me."

As I say it, I'm filled with such a longing to be back in my tiny room with my wooden crib bed under the square skylight where I can see the stars.

Even school, here in the vast stretches of fjords and mountains, seems somehow manageable. I can think about it with a new kind of clarity. A week in school and weekends in the forest to recharge. It doesn't seem like such a bad deal.

Mum winds her scarf up round her face to help cut out the chill. "You're not too cold? We could always go below deck to warm up."

I shake my head. There's no way I'm missing this last voyage.

*Goodbye, Ulya,* I whisper over the water. She won't hear me. She's gone now. She's set free, I hope. Maybe she took that rainbow bridge up to the stars and is part of those magical green lights.

There are still ghosts here on Svalbard. There are ghosts everywhere. The whales that should still be swimming these waters. But they're coming back, and will keep coming back, swimming in from the edge of the world.

Icy water splashes into my face, and I gasp with the shock of the cold, as a huge grey form leaps out of the water, its gigantic head breaking through the ice.

A bowhead.

I could reach out to touch it. From the depths of the sea, a creature of the true north.

A cloud of fishy breath surrounds us.

I grasp for the phone in my pocket, to take a photo, but I know it's already too late. The whale's gone, back down to its icy world.

It doesn't matter, I have it in my heart, that I looked into the eye of a bowhead. All power, beauty and serenity. One of the ancient ones, the slow swimmers of the Arctic Ocean.

It glides off starboard, and Mum and I don't say a thing. We huddle against each other, and drift on the swell that takes us home.

# Author's Note

This book is set in Pyramiden, a former Soviet coal-mining settlement in Svalbard, halfway between Norway and the North Pole. The settlement was named after the pyramid-shaped mountain that looms over it.

Miners lived in block-style housing, with rounded edges to curb the Arctic wind. Despite subzero temperatures and twenty-four hour darkness in winter, it was a prestigious place to be employed and whole families made their lives here. A communist 'utopia', Pyramiden boasted grand buildings, including a Palace of Culture, with concert hall, ballet studio, basketball court and library. There was a heated swimming pool, a football pitch and a large cafeteria where everyone had their meals. It was home to the world's northernmost primary school and the northernmost grand piano too.

After the last coal was extracted in 1998, Pyramiden became a ghost town. The Soviet Union had collapsed and coal-mining in such a remote place wasn't profitable. There had also been a terrible accident. In 1996, a plane from Moscow crashed whilst attempting to land in bad weather, killing all 141 people on board, including three children. This was about ten per cent of Pyramiden's entire population. Morale in the town and the mining company plummeted and the decision was made to close operations. The final residents left in October 1998, before the winter darkness set in.

Today the town is trapped in time, largely preserved as it was in the icy conditions of Svalbard. Besides birds and Arctic foxes, it's home to a few solitary caretakers and is visited each year by a handful of curious tourists, and polar bears! I haven't been – or at least I've only been in my imagination, researching and writing this book – but it's endlessly intriguing to me.

Pyramiden is an amazing setting for a story, but I have taken a degree of creative licence (and no doubt made some mistakes as well!), so this is my version of the town. Do look up photos of the real place. It's like looking at another world!

This is my Svalbard too, but some books I found helpful in imagining it were the guidebook *Spitsbergen – Svalbard* by Rolf Stange (also his brilliant website www.spitsbergen-svalbard.com); *Ice Rivers* by Jemma Wadham; *The Library of Ice* by Nancy Campbell;

*A Woman in the Polar Night* by Christiane Ritter; *Arctic Dreams* by Barry Lopez.

Svalbard does not have an indigenous population, but in my book Mikkal's parents are Sami and originate from Northern Scandinavia. I loved looking at Erika Larsen's photography collection, *Sami – Walking with Reindeer.*

# Thanks to

At the end of December 1999, I travelled with a group of university friends to Northern Finland. We spent a happy few days in a remote cabin above the Arctic Circle welcoming in 2000. Walking in the forest, playing in the snow, watching the northern lights, warming ourselves in the sauna and mostly failing to make the jump into the icy plunge pool afterwards (obviously, Lizzy, you did). I knew I was both in a very special place in its own right, and close to the edge of other, wilder places, further north. I loved it. And the night train! And the amazing Arktikum museum in Rovaniemi! Thank you, everyone on that trip, but especially Dan Wood for making it happen, and Pera for your hut. Thanks also to the Finland 2019 crew for our twenty-year-later reunion, with added young people. That was so much fun, and my kids' favourite holiday. Anyway, those trips are the sum total of my Arctic experience, and don't really qualify me to write about Svalbard, but they made me yearn for the far north and helped bring me to this idea.

Cecilia Blomdahl is a videographer living and working in Longyearbyen. Watching her vlogs with coffee every morning became a favourite writing ritual. Thank you, Cecilia! And lovely Grim too!

The artist Emma Stibbon. In the absence of a research trip, a conversation with Emma helped make journeying to Svalbard come alive for me. Please look up her work. She's amazing at capturing icy landscapes! Thanks to Helen Waters for putting us in touch.

Michelle Paver for introducing me to Spitsbergen and writing the scariest book I've ever read, *Dark Matter*!

The community of readers I'm lucky enough to encounter on Twitter, Instagram and sometimes in real life, including booksellers, teachers, librarians and bloggers. Your reviews and support put my books into the hands of new readers and I'm always grateful. And to my young readers – I wouldn't be writing at all if you weren't reading my books. It's one of the biggest honours in my life that you do.

Writing friends, especially my loyal Swaggers, and also Julia Tuffs, for sharing the highs and lows of this journey. Thanks, Sita Brahmachari, for our walks and for spurring me on. And indeed all my friends and family – for support, distraction, encouragement and so much more.

The sustainability working group at the Society of Authors, particularly Hannah Gold, Philip Kavvadias and

Piers Torday (who leads it with such dedication). You bring me back to what's important and are beacons of hope and change. Also Lauren James for setting up the Climate Fiction League and spreading our message.

As always, more thanks than I can say to Dom, Matilda, Daisy, Freddie and Bea. Particular thanks to Dom for reading at the last hour and finding mistakes. Also for suggesting the idea of a community left behind in Pyramiden in the first place. Everything else followed on from that.

Gillie Russell, my agent. I love that your emails always come with a burst of sea air and encouragement!

Artist Kate Forrester and designer Pip Johnson for this breathtakingly beautiful cover! I saw it in the early stages and it's no exaggeration to say it kept me writing and urged me to make my book better.

Little Tiger! For everything you do to get my books out into the world! Particularly Dannie Price (I'm so grateful for your kindness and enthusiasm), Lauren Ace, Kat Cassidy, George Hanratty, Summer Lanchester, Demet Hoffmeyer, Nicola O'Connell and Sarah Shaffi. Thanks to Lucy Rogers for first-class copyediting and Anna Bowles for eagle-eyed proofreading.

Lastly, my awesome editor, Mattie Whitehead. Thanks for pushing this book on and helping shape it when I was lost in the wilderness. You were the midnight sun in my polar night!

# WHERE

*the*

# WORLD

*turns*

# WILD

## Nicola Penfold

# Praise for Where the World Turns Wild

"A sense of the natural world's curative power runs
through this adventurous story like a seam of gold."
Guardian

★

"Some books are excellent story telling, and some books broaden
your knowledge and mind, and some just ought to
be written and this book is all three. I loved it."
Hilary McKay, author of *The Skylarks' War*

★

"A brilliant adventure that pulls you headlong into Juniper and
Bear's world, where survival depends upon finding the wild."
Gill Lewis, author of *Sky Hawk*

★

"A fabulous debut with a powerful ecological message."
AM Howell, author of *The Garden of Lost Secrets*

★

"A truly heartfelt and very striking novel."
Darren Simpson, author of *Scavengers*

★

"A beautiful, memorable story about all the important things –
love, family, loyalty and courage."
Sinéad O'Hart, author of *The Eye of the North*

★

"Wondrous, warm-hearted, wildly exhilarating."
Nizrana Farook, author of *The Girl Who Stole an Elephant*

★

"This compelling book has future classic written all over it!"
Lindsay Galvin, author of *The Secret Deep*

★

"This novel packs a powerful punch."
Cath Howe, author of *Ella on the Outside*

"Bold and beautiful"
Sita Brahmachari

# BETWEEN

# SEA

# and

# SKY

*Nicola Penfold*

# PRAISE FOR *BETWEEN SEA AND SKY*

"A message to us all in the most powerful, evocative and hopeful story spinning."
Hilary McKay, author of *The Skylarks' War*

★

"A beautifully told adventure that will have readers, like its protagonists, diving deep to discover the fragility of our eco-system and emerging emboldened to protect its delicate balance."
Sita Brahmachari, author of *Where the River Runs Gold*

★

"Breathtaking, transporting and captivating.
I was absolutely hooked."
Polly Ho-Yen, author of *Boy in the Tower*

★

"BOSS level MG dystopia, so vivid!"
Louie Stowell, author of *The Dragon in the Library*

★

"Nicola Penfold makes me want to love our planet harder, hold it closer."
Rashmi Sirdeshpande, author of *How to Change the World*

★

"A rising star of children's fiction, mixing a thrilling evocative adventure with pertinent themes of the environment and recovery."
Fiona Noble, *The Bookseller*

★

"This is compelling, high-stakes storytelling. I stayed up late turning the pages and this will be a favourite that I will return to over and over again."
Nizrana Farook, author of *The Girl Who Stole an Elephant*

★

"A powerful call to protect the world we've got."
Sinéad O'Hart, author of *The Eye of the North*

★

"Atmospheric, memorable, extraordinarily gripping, this is storytelling at its finest."
*Guardian*

Read on for an extract from

# BETWEEN
# SEA
## *and*
# SKY

# ONE
## Nat

The dares have started early this year. Normally we wait till summer, but there are still two weeks of school to go and coloured flags are already appearing around the bay. Like everyone got bored at the same time.

It's a trail. You put the flag someplace you shouldn't go. The marshes or shoreline, or ground still saturated with poisons from way back. Mostly it's the solar fields. The fields of silicon panels that have been our playground since we were five, even though they're strictly no access.

The flags are calling cards. Proof you've been where you say you've been. Then you dare someone else to go and get them.

I call on Lucas at 8 a.m. sharp. He's in the apartment next to me and Mum, on the top floor. *The most stairs*, Tally says when we leave her behind on the first floor.

*The best view*, we retort. *Yeah, of the solar fields*, she'll fling back at us.

"Flag day! Flag day!" I chant through Lucas's letter box. The door swings open into my face.

"Watch it!" he says, stepping out in front of me. "You want my parents to hear?"

"You're joking, aren't you?" I say. "No grown-ups would be awake this time on a Sunday! Mum says her eyes need to be shut for twelve hours straight after a week in the growing tower!"

Lucas smiles good-naturedly. The growing tower is the heart of Edible Uplands, the crop-growing complex where most of the adults in the compound work their shifts. Vegetable and salad plants stacked up in rows in a pink incubating light. Mum says it's like looking into a permanent sunset, especially since Central District upped their quotas again. Sometimes I wonder if they need the extra food at all. Maybe it's stacked in warehouses somewhere, rotting, and all they really want is to show their power over us.

Lucas and I spring down the concrete stairwell. We always take it three steps at a time.

"Tally?" Lucas asks at the first floor.

"She'll be at the bike sheds already," I say, swinging past him and leaping down to the ground floor.

Tally whistles when she sees me. "Nat! Mate! You've not

chickened out then?"

I shake my head, fast. Tally, Lucas and I have flagged together since nursery and today it's my turn to place the flag. A red one. Everyone uses red for their hardest dares. It's meant to be someplace dangerous, that's the point, but we've always left Billy Crier's windmill alone.

"We need to up the stakes. You said it," I say.

"*We've only got two years left, but we're still playing baby games,*" Tally had said at lunch yesterday. I'd known straight away where I'd have to go.

At some point kids stop with the daring. They get pulled into work at Edible Uplands or the desalination plant. Or inland – some assignment will come up at the polytunnels or one of the factories. We've got to make the most of our time together.

"Least there's no wind," Lucas says. I take a gulp of air. It's hot, with the lingering taste of salt. It hasn't rained in weeks.

Tally leads the way out of the compound. We live in four floors of concrete and steel, on stilted metal legs. Like some spacecraft landed years ago to refuel but never managed to lift off again. The legs have been surrounded by seawater so many times during floods that they're starting to corrode.

Even the concrete's cracking now, imploding from the inside. They built it cheap, Mum says. They didn't reckon on the wind and the heat and the salt. They should have built it further back – it's too close to the sea.

"It's not too late to change the plan," Lucas continues, looking back at me. "Your mum won't want extra points."

We're standing under the board where all compound families are listed and where civil disobedience points go up against the names. For shirking shifts or missing quotas or going over the boundary, or a long list of other things Central deem impermissible.

Even when everyone's been compliant, peacekeepers still come from Central every so often to take away the top offender for the prison ship. It's a deterrent and reminder. Never forget the rules.

"Mischa better watch out," Tal says, whistling. "His dad's three off the top."

I hate that list. Our friends and neighbours, their names blur together when I look.

"We won't dare Mischa," I say quickly. "Not this time."

"Or Eli," Lucas cuts in. "His family's not far behind."

Tal shakes her head. "Nah. Sara and Luna, that's who we'll pick. Their families barely have any points at all. Those girls know how not to get caught."

"We could always do fifth field instead. We haven't done that in ages," Lucas says. He's still trying to give me an escape, but there's no way I'm backing out now. Not in front of Tal.

"Where's the fun in that?" Tally's already saying. "Fifth

field is just like first field, and second and third." She lets her voice drone on for emphasis.

"No," I say, determined. "It's Billy Crier's windmill. Just like we said."

"Cool," Tally says breezily, and lifts her bike down the last few steps.

The mirrored fields dazzle you when you come out from the compound's shadow. Fields of silicon stretching away either side of Drylands Road, until everything becomes sky. There's shortages of most things round here, but sky we have in abundance.

Most people went inland during the floods. When the seawaters rose, they drowned whole villages and towns, sweeping people right off the edge of the earth, spreading disease and famine. But some people were brought back to the bay after, when the wind pumps were working again, draining seawater out of the land. Edible Uplands and the solar fields were built, and our compound, with its housing, service shops and school. Those are the things our district is known for. Them and the prison ship, brooding out on the horizon, representing everything bad about the sea.

"Race you!" Tally calls, jumping on her bike, and Lucas and I ride after her, our bike tyres cartwheeling over the maintenance tracks.

Even when there's no wind, there's something. Energy, from the ground maybe. It builds in the rotating wheels and passes up into you.

We leave our bikes stashed under one of the panels in third field. We make sure they're hidden, so no one recognizes them as ours.

I used to love these fields. It was a novelty to be out of the compound at all and we'd spend whole days tramping through them. The fields felt alive – electrons bouncing round the silicon panels, taking sunlight, parcelling it up into electricity. It's pretty miraculous. The shine just wears off after a bit.

"Looks like we're clear," Tally says, scanning the field either side. We have to be careful. If you're caught in the fields, it's one civil disobedience point. Points for minors go up against your parents. You only get your own chart when you start your shifts. No one wants to risk their parents being sent to that ship, to spend the rest of their days at sea.

We proceed on foot, single file between the panels. Tally first, then me, then Lucas.

We've flagged most places there are to flag already. All around the harbour, Customs and Immigration and Edible Uplands. Last year a flag was left at the top of the growing tower and all the kids in the compound were grounded for a month. Every single one, because no one would break ranks and say who it was that had climbed the rickety ladder. Flag rivalries aside, growing up in the compound makes you pretty tight.

Billy Crier's windmill isn't like the growing tower. The danger isn't just in the climb.

It's older than the other wind pumps. It predates not only the floods and the Hunger Years, but the Decline, and even the Greedy Years before that. It's from when the land was still healthy enough to farm, before the poisons and the saltwater got in.

"It's just a story. He was probably never even real," Lucas says, as the windmill looms closer, black and broken.

"Yeah?" I say, looking back.

Lucas nods emphatically. "Dad says they only tell about Billy Crier to keep us out of the fields."

"Liar," Tally pronounces, staring back at him defiantly.

Lucas blushes. "Well, the ghost bit at least."

"I guess Nat's going to find out," Tally says, crooking her neck ghoulishly and making an eerie kind of cry.

# About the Author

**Nicola Penfold** was born in Billinge and grew up in Doncaster. She studied English at Cambridge University. Nicola has worked in a reference library and for a health charity, but being a writer was always the job she wanted most. She is the author of *Between Sea and Sky* and *Where the World Turns Wild*, which was chosen as a Future Classic for the BookTrust School Library Pack. Nicola writes in the coffee shops and green spaces of North London, where she lives with her husband, four children and three cats, and escapes when she can to wilder corners of the UK for adventures.